The Wives of Elm Street

— THE THIRD NOVEL —

To all my wonderful friends
at v. salta.
Thanks for friendship and
support and loads of fun.
Darla

DARLENE J. FORBES

Fulton Books, Inc.
Meadville, PA

Published by Fulton Books 2021

ISBN 978-1-63710-702-7 (paperback)
ISBN 978-1-63710-703-4 (digital)

Printed in the United States of America

To my great bocce team for their loyalty and support,
Starr, Gary, Virginia, Ted, Angela, Bill, and Mario.

CHAPTER 1

Best Friends

Bocce practice was scheduled for five on Tuesdays; game nights were every Thursday night, starting at six, and Maggie and Joan were running late again for practice. The ladies played two seasons, fall to winter and spring to summer, with three weeks off between each season. Bocce is a huge, competitive sport in the small town of St. Helena, California. This quaint little town is at the heart of wine country, located in Napa Valley. Joan laughingly told Maggie to slow down. "We're only five minutes late, and I'd rather walk than ride with you. And speaking of late, why were you late again?"

Maggie apologized and told Joan that her relief pharmacist was late again, which put her behind, adding, "The others can practice until we get there." Barb and Susie usually drove themselves as did the other four team members. The eight team members tried to get together at least once a week to practice.

The four best friends, Maggie, Barb, Susie, and Joan, had been on the team for eight years. They were casual friends with the other four members of the team, Nancy, Chris, Judy, and Margie, but the four besties had started the team and enjoyed spending time together. After the bocce game, the four women would frequently go to a local pub for a glass of wine and shared gossip. The other four members seldom joined the little clique; although when asked, they usually declined, often feeling the invite wasn't sincere. The four best friends had been very close for years and were very protective of their friendship.

When Maggie and Joan arrived at practice, the other team members were already throwing balls on the court. Depending on how practice went, team-captain Barb would decide which four would start the game on Thursday night, and which four would play the second game, and the same for the third game. Bocce only needs four members to play the three games, two members on each end playing against the opponents of two at the other end. Barb always tried to use all eight members of the team for at least one game. Other teams may have all men on their teams, and some were a combination of men and women. The rules of the game were the same for all teams; three games of twelve points and whoever reaches twelve first is the winner. The game is similar to lawn bowling with four red balls and four green balls and a small white ball called the *pallino*. The goal is the player that gets their red or green ball closest to the pallino is the winner, and the game can go quickly or slowly depending on the skill level of the player and the team. Each team is assigned a color, red or green, by flipping a coin.

After an hour of practice, the teams called it a night and went home to their families to cook dinner, help with homework, or just relax. The four women promised they would get together after Thursday night's game and have a glass of wine at one of the cozy restaurants or bars in town. St. Helena is famous for its great food and wine, and the women tried to pick a new spot each week.

The four friends all lived on Elm Street, within blocks of each other. Susie and Joan lived on the same block three houses apart, and Maggie and Barb lived just two blocks from the other two, six houses apart. St. Helena is a small town with just four stoplights, and everything is within walking distance. Barb and Susie grew up in St. Helena and had gone to elementary and high school together, and they had been friends since the third grade. Barb had grown up on Pine Street, and Susie's Parents had lived on Spring Street. Maggie and her family had moved to St. Helena when Tom, Maggie's husband, had joined a dental practice. Joan and her family had moved to town for Joan's husband's hardware store business.

Each of the women had busy careers as well as husbands and children. Maggie is forty-nine and is a pharmacist at the only pharmacy in town, and her husband Tom is a dentist. They have two sons: Michael, twenty-two, and Jeff, sixteen. Maggie and Tom met at college at Davis and had moved to St. Helena twenty-two years ago for Tom's dental practice, and Maggie had quickly found a job at the pharmacy. Their son Michael is a senior at Sacramento State College, and Jeff is a sophomore at St. Helena High School. Maggie is very pretty, with blond-streaked hair, blue eyes, and is the tallest of the women at five feet nine. Maggie is on the thin side but curvy where it counts. Maggie has been fending off males since she was fifteen.

Barb is forty-five and is a teacher at the elementary school, and her husband Jack is a vineyard manager with one of the larger wine growers in the valley. They have three daughters: Rachel, eight; Brenda, thirteen; and Lacey, sixteen. Barb had met Jack at the small county fair in town, which they both attend. Barb would describe herself as kind of attractive, five feet five, dark brown hair with brown eyes and dimples. She would like to lose ten pounds, but then who wouldn't?

Susie is forty-six and is a winemaker in a small boutique winery, and her husband Mark is a stockbroker in San Francisco. Susie and Mark have one son, Greg, fifteen. Greg is a sophomore at St. Helena High School.

Mark commutes to San Francisco three to four days a week. Susie can be described as gorgeous, sexy, five feet seven with natural blond hair and green eyes. Susie is very aware of how attractive she is and uses it to her every advantage.

Joan is fifty and is a nurse at the local hospital, and her husband Bob owns the local hardware store. They have two children: Brad, twenty-four, and Sandy, eighteen. They moved to St. Helena fifteen years ago from Ohio when Bob's uncle died, leaving the hardware store to Bob. Brad is on his own and living in Napa, working at one of the high-end hotels as a bartender. Sandy is attending the local college in St. Helena, studying nursing. Joan is not beautiful but pretty in a cute, perky way. Joan has auburn hair with blue eyes and is maybe five feet three if she stands very straight, and she maintains a trim figure by careful eating and running the halls of the hospital.

The four women had met through a book club twelve years ago, and their friendship has developed and grown stronger through the years. Their husbands like each other, and the couples socialize several times a month. Their children that are close in ages are friends, and Maggie's son Jeff and Susie's son Greg are good buddies. They are a tight-knit group that has seen each other through some very tough times. But even the best of friends have secrets, things they can't talk about, secrets that the others might not understand, so each woman kept some of her thoughts and secrets to herself.

Maggie

Thursday night, Maggie rushed home from the pharmacy to put on a pair of jeans and a warm sweater for bocce; the fall evening was turning chilly. She told her husband Tom and son Jeff that they could either order pizzas, or she would fix soup and sandwiches when she got home from bocce, but she warned them that it could be as late as nine when she got home. The more difficult the game, the longer it could take, point by point, and the gals normally went for a glass of wine after the game.

Tom gave Maggie a dismissive look and told her that he was getting a little tired of her being gone two to three nights a week, and he would like a normal dinner once in a while. Tom said, "I'll order pizza, but I'm pretty dammed sick of this schedule and you spending so much f——king time with your buds. I think you care more about your friends and teammates that you do me and the boys."

Maggie replied, "Look, Tom, I don't want to fight, but you play golf every Saturday morning with your guy friends. And once a month you have a poker night, and I don't give you a bad time. So lay off me for God's sakes." She then gave Tom a quick wave and ran into Jeff's room to give him a hug and told him to finish his homework.

While Maggie was driving to bocce, she thought to herself that Tom had been more distant and nastier to her lately. *What was that about? I'll ask the girls if their husbands are giving them a bad time. Or is just my husband being a jerk? I work hard all week, take care of the house, and cook most nights and try to be supportive of Tom when he has late patients. Give me a break, I do 60 percent, and he barely does 40 percent. What does he expect, a slave?*

By the time Maggie got to the bocce courts, she had started to calm down and put this little disagreement with Tom behind her. Maggie was paired with Barb for the first game, and she quickly got caught up in the game. She sat out the second game and played the third game with Joan. Their team only had seven players that night. Maggie's team won two out of three games and were in good spirits when they finished at eight fifteen and headed for one of their favorite haunts for a glass of wine.

When the four women found a quiet table and placed their wine order, they started going over the three games and what mistakes they had made to lose the second game. Barb said, "I think it's my fault. I lost my attention. I was just off a bit, my groove just wasn't there."

"No," Maggie said, "it just happened we can't win them all, although we'd like to."

The other three women agreed, and Joan said, "There's no saying you're sorry in bocce, it's a team effort." Everyone laughed, and the subject changed.

Maggie asked the three women if their husbands ever gave them a bad time about their time away from home, either for bocce or for other activities. She told them that Tom had been a real ass about her leaving tonight, and she was getting a little sick of his attitude.

Joan thought about it and told them, "No, Bob never says anything, and he often comes home later than I do. He's usually at the hardware store until after 8:00 p.m. and sometimes later. I'm normally the one that's pissed off when he's late for dinner and the food gets cold and I end up eating alone."

Joan worked the six to three shift at the hospital, and she was up and gone before Bob woke up and had to go to bed by ten, so they didn't see a lot of each other. Their daughter Sandy was seldom home for dinner but usually out with friends, and Brad lived in Napa with his friend, so they were lucky if they saw him once or twice a month.

Susie jumped in on the conversation and told them that Mark often stayed overnight in San Francisco, so she was alone several evenings a week. Her son Greg would fend for himself when Susie wasn't home and would make a sandwich or pick up fast food. Greg had football practice several afternoons a week, and he didn't care if his mom was home at night. Greg had gotten used to Susie's hours and knew doing crush or other busy seasons at the winery that Susie would be having late hours, and he would often eat with his friends or make a sandwich. As most teenagers, Greg cared more for his own interests than his parents'.

Barb also spoke up that Jack often worked later than she did in the vineyards, so he didn't dare complain about Barb's hours. Being a teacher, Barb had the most regular hours, other than a few late nights when she held open house nights for parents or had specific meetings. Otherwise, she was home and provided a good meal four to five nights a week for her family. Barb continued that Jack was pretty easygoing and didn't much care what he ate or when he ate; she didn't want to give any more details as to why Jack didn't care about eating. Barb's friends thought that Jack was a good guy, and she was glad to let them think that.

Susie told Maggie not to let Tom's attitude get under her skin. She would mention Tom's behavior to her husband, Mark, since the guys played golf together and ask him to find out what Tom's real issues were. Susie patted Maggie's hand, and said, "Tom is usually such an easygoing guy, maybe something at the office is bothering him. I'm sure he'll calm down."

*****

The four women then changed the subject to their children, their work, and the always-crowded streets in St. Helena, especially during the heavy tourist season. The locals had learned all the back streets to get around town and had learned to avoid the main street running right through town. It could take fifteen to twenty minutes to drive four miles through town or more. The locals loved the income from the tourists but also hated the crowded streets, stores, and restaurants. The wineries were a huge draw to the valley, and tourism just continued to grow.

After an hour, the women decided to call it a night and agreed they would see each other the following Saturday night for a dinner party at Joan's house. The couples tried to host a small dinner party once a month and alternated at each other's homes. St. Helena is a small, tight town, and the locals tended to stay within their own social circles.

Barb

When Barb and Jack were dressing to go to Joan and Bob's house for dinner, Barb looked at Jack and asked him to please behave tonight. "Don't drink too much. Please don't make a fool of yourself. You know how nasty you get when you drink too much. I love you and care about you, but sometimes I just don't respect you. Please just pace yourself tonight."

Jack gave Barb a nasty look and responded, "Yes, Barb, I will be your puppet. I'll just have a couple of drinks and behave myself. God knows I wouldn't want to embarrass you or damage your perfect reputation as the goody-goody among your friends."

Barb went into the bathroom to put on her makeup and sat down on the edge of the bathtub and buried her head in her hands and cried. She thought back to when she had met Jack seventeen years ago at the local county fair. They had both been standing in line for a ride on the Ferris wheel, and they got paired together on the ride and began chatting during the seven-minute ride. Barb's friend Judy had backed out at the last minute, claiming a fear of heights, and Jack being next in line offered to ride with Barb. At the time Barb thought it was very charming, and when the ride ended and Jack asked Barb for her phone number, she was glad to give it to him.

Jack told Barb that he had just moved to St. Helena from Washington State to be a vineyard manager for one of the larger wineries in the valley. He told Barb that he hadn't made any friends yet and was eager to get involved in the local social scene. Barb had been twenty-seven when she met Jack, and she was ready to settle down and start a family. She had dated a bit after finishing college, but being on the shy side, she did not warm up to men easily, so when she met Jack, she was ripe for the picking.

Barb had been leery of marriage after witnessing her parents' stormy marriage. Her father had been an abusive alcoholic, and she had seen what this disastrous marriage had done to her mother and her little sister. Her mother was old before her time and had given up on life and died by she was in her midfifties. Barb felt that her mother had willed her own death to escape her abusive and cruel husband. Barb's father had died of cirrhosis of the liver just four years later. Barb had gone to college, and her younger sister, Pam, had joined the Peace Corps.

After dating Jack for six months, Barb felt like she had met the man of her dreams. He was well educated, well behaved and, if not handsome, nice looking, slim, and well groomed. The thing most important to Barb was that Jack did not seem to be much of a drinker. He would have a glass of wine or two with dinner As Barb did, but Jack never seemed to overindulge. He did, however, drink a ton of coffee. One night, after several months of dating, Barb asked Jack if he ever had a drinking problem since he drank so much coffee. She apologized but explained about her father being an alcoholic, and that she could never be involved with a man that had a drinking problem. She was very blunt, that she could not go through life with an alcoholic again.

Jack had just given Barb a hug and told her not to worry, but he really didn't like the taste or the effects of alcohol and really wasn't much of a drinker, so not to worry, she was safe with him. Barb had been so relieved at the time, and she was surer about her feelings for Jack than ever. When Jack proposed a few months later, Barb was ecstatic and quickly agreed.

They planned a small wedding at the local Catholic church and a reception at the St. Helena community center. Barb asked her Sister Pam and her good friend Susie to stand up with her, and Jack asked an old friend from Washington and one of his new friends from the winery to be his groomsmen. The wedding was lovely, with a catered dinner from a local barbecue restaurant and then dancing and music provided by a local favored DJ. The happy couple would then spend five days in a small B&B in Carmel.

When Barb and Jack returned to St. Helena, they moved into Barb's small rental house until they could save the money to buy their first home in St. Helena. Barb felt like she couldn't be happier—until three weeks after the wedding when Jack became nasty and belligerent for no reason and started a fight with Barb over nothing. They had finished dinner and were having a second glass of wine when, out of the blue, Jack got angry over some imagined slight and proceeded to yell at Barb, calling her filthy names and telling her how sorry he was that he had ever married her.

Barb was absolutely floored; she could not begin to understand what had just happened. Had Jack been drinking more than she had noticed? The dinner had been good, and she just didn't understand why Jack was so angry at her. He had always been so loving and kind. Who was this man? It was like Dr. Jekyll and Mr. Hyde. Barb burst into tears and went to bed, where she cried herself to sleep. She never knew when Jack came to bed.

The next morning, Jack woke up and gave Barb a big kiss and proceeded to make love to her. Barb was completely confused. Had she imagined last night and the awful things Jack had said? No, she was sure of what had happened. She turned to Jack and asked what had happened last night, why out of the blue he had turned ugly and mean and said terrible things to her.

Jack seemed confused and said he didn't remember any fight, or having said anything to her, and she must have misunderstood him. He told her that he loved her and would never deliberately hurt her feelings. Maybe he had drunk one more glass of wine that he should have, and if so he was sorry, and it would never happen again. They made love, and all was forgiven if not forgotten, especially by Barb.

This happened several more times over the next few months, with Jack getting angry over nothing, screaming at Barb, making accusations, and then being sorry the next morning. Barb was beginning to think that she was going crazy; had she made a terrible mistake, marrying Jack after only eight months? Barb thought about a divorce, but she was beginning to suspect that she was pregnant.

Barb was beginning to feel trapped. She told Jack that if he didn't stop drinking, she would leave him, baby or no baby. Jack was delighted about being a father and promised he would do better; if he had a drink, it would only be one or two glasses of wine to be social but would not go to excess. Jack had kept his word through the pregnancy and had turned out to be a kind and loving father.

As Barb sat in the bathroom, she thought back to all the good times and all the bad times that Jack had not kept his promise, and had railed at her and the girls. Each time she had threatened to leave him, Jack would promise to do better and would be good for six or eight months, and then he would be at it again.

Oh please, God, Barb thought, *let him behave tonight. I always feel like I'm walking on eggshells and so do the girls.*

When Barb and Jack left the house, Barb reminded Lacey to take good care of her younger sisters, Rachel and Brenda, and to order pizza and watch movies. They didn't have a set bedtime since the next day was Sunday.

CHAPTER 4

Susie

When Susie and Mark were driving over to Joan and Bob's house for dinner, Susie asked Mark how his week had gone. She told Mark that since he'd stay in the city two or three nights a week, the only time they had together was the weekends. "Your son Greg sometimes wonders if he has a father. Greg would love it if you went to his after-school sports events, or if you would take the time to spend some father-son time with him." Susie continued, "The last few months, you have made yourself less and less available to both of us."

Mark said, "Look, Susie, the market has not been going well, and I'm busting my hump to keep you and our son living in the custom that you both seem to enjoy. So back off and just leave me the hell alone."

He continued, "I'm going to our friends tonight for dinner, and I will put a good face on it, but don't push me. They're more your friends than mine, and I don't feel the need to spend as much time with them as you do. The only one I enjoy and have something in common with is Tom. We enjoy our golf games, but we don't get into each other's business."

Susie looked at Mark and asked him, "What do you think happened to us? We used to be so close, and we did everything together. We shared our dreams, and we built a good life. What happened? I just don't understand."

Mark just shrugged off Susie's question and told her, "Life got in the way, Susie. We both have stressful, busy lives, and we are doing the best we can. Life is not always blissful and exciting, but some-times more boring than exciting. Don't make a big deal out of it, we're doing okay. Let's not examine the whole marriage thing. It is what it is. Just take it as it comes."

By the time they had arrived at Joan and Bob's house, the air was thick with their silence. Both Susie and Mark had receded back into their own thoughts. Mark was thinking, *Why the hell can't Susie back off and stop trying to analyze our life and just roll with it? I'm not her lapdog, and she needs to give me a break.*

Susie was thinking, Why do I bother trying to reach Mark? I should just live my life however the hell I feel like.

She and Mark had not had a good sex life for months; they either ignored it, or it was so automatic that neither got any pleasure from it.

Susie and Mark were greeted with hugs from Joan and Bob, as they hung up their coats and said hello to the others in the room. Mark pulled Bob aside and said, "Make me a drink. I've had a hard week between work and Susie." Bob led Mark over to the bar setup in the dining room and gave Bob his choice of wine or something a little stronger. Bob asked Mark if he wanted to talk about it, but Mark just shook his head and said, "That's the last thing I want is to talk, but thanks."

Susie was surrounded and hugged by her friends, Joan, Maggie, and Barb. Maggie thought Susie looked a little off or sad, and asked Susie if she was all right. Susie told the ladies she was fine, but that her husband and all men can be such butts. She told her friends that she and Mark were just drifting farther apart, and she was getting to the point that she didn't care anymore if they stayed together or not. She said, "He's cold and distant most of the time to me and Greg. I'm beginning to wonder if he's cheating, or if something else is going on."

Maggie told the ladies that Tom had been like that every now and then, complaining and cold. She thought it might just be a male thing, midlife crisis. She said, "I just try to ignore his bad moods and hope for the better days. I'm sure we'll all survive it, and at least we have each other."

The four women then joined the men for dinner. The dinner had been delicious; the compliments to Joan's lasagna was impressive. The rest of the evening went well, with a game of charades ending the evening. The guests started departing at eleven, with thanks and promises by the ladies to see each other in a few days for bocce practice.

As Mark and Susie drove home, Mark commented, "Well, are you happy? I was my usual pleasant, kiss-ass self. I did my marital social duties, so I warn you that I may not be as available for future social activities. I'm going to need to spend more time at work. The market is very volatile right now, and I need to put all my efforts into my work. Susie, what I'm basically saying is that you may need to attend some of these activities alone, and I don't want to hear you whining about it."

Susie told Mark, "Fine. I'm glad to occupy myself, and I can certainly find things to keep myself busy. I will tell Greg that his dad just doesn't have time for him anymore. In my opinion, a fifteen-year-old boy needs his dad more than ever with questions and bonding that a mother cannot always provide. But forget it, I totally understand. You just don't give a damn."

They drove home in silence, and each went to bed claiming their own side of the bed, without a good-night kiss or hug. Susie looked in on Greg in his room to say good night, and just be grateful that he was such a good kid. She felt lucky that at least one man in her life was a good, kind, and caring person.

CHAPTER 5

Joan

Joan and Bob chatted about the evening as they stacked and loaded the dishwasher. Bob told Joan that her dinner was outstanding as usual and that the charades had been a good idea, since some of their friends seemed to be a little uptight or more subdued than normal. Bob asked Joan, "Was it my imagination, or did you notice a strained atmosphere between Susie and Mark? I also thought that Barb seemed on edge, and I caught her watching Jack a lot. Is something going on with these guys that I don't know about?"

Joan had noticed that her friends had seemed a little tense, but she wasn't quite sure what was going on. She told Bob, "I think they're fine, just the normal marital blues that occur after so many years of marriage. Couples can get bored with each other, and sometimes they just need to hit the refresh button." She herself sometimes felt that she had growing pains, and often wished that Bob was more exciting, and more sophisticated like Tom or Mark. Bob was so steady, a good husband and a great father, but still boring. Often all they talked about was the hardware store, literally nuts and bolts, and his loyal customers.

They went upstairs to check on Sandy, who had been out with friends, and then retired to their own bedroom. Bob was feeling amorous and turned to Joan the minute they climbed into bed. Joan didn't feel like making love after cleaning and cooking all afternoon, but she also didn't want to disappoint Bob, so she would just comply and let her mind wander to other more pleasant thoughts. More and more their love life was automatic, no excitement, and nothing new, just same old.

As soon as Bob was finished, he turned over and was snoring within five minutes. Joan lay awake for hours after Bob were asleep, wondering where their romance had gone. When they had met back in Ohio after college, Bob had been so charming and had pursued her with flowers, candy, and romantic love notes. Where had that guy gone? Bob had once dreamed of being a lawyer, and he had been almost through law school when his uncle died and left him the hardware store. Bob's parents had convinced him to take over the store and the small inheritance that his uncle had left him. There are so many lawyers already, and the hardware store was a sure thing, an established business, and Bob and his parents felt that he couldn't turn it down.

Sunday morning, as Joan was making breakfast for the three of them, their son Brad walked into the kitchen and said, "Hi, Mom, am I too late to join you guys for breakfast?"

Joan said, "Absolutely not. There is always room for you, and it's been weeks since we saw you." Brad told his mom that he had bought a new motorcycle, and he wanted to try it out on the trail between Napa and St. Helena.

"Oh Brad," Joan said, "I hate motorcycles. I see all these terrible accident victims at the hospital. Young people either die every day or are severely maimed by crazy souped-up bikes. Sorry, but I love you. And I don't want you crippled or dead."

"Oh Mom," Brad replied, "I'm always careful and wear my helmet. Don't worry, I'll be fine. You're just being my mom, I can handle the bike."

Bob walked into the kitchen while Brad was making his point to his mom. Bob gave his son a huge hug and said, "What did I hear about my son buying a bike"?

Joan looked at Bob and gave him a pleading look, begging him to convince Brad to give up on the bike. Bob walked over to Joan, rubbed her back, and told her to lay off the kid, that boys and men like bikes, and he was sure his son could handle the bike. Bob just reminded Brad to always wear his helmet and be cautious on the trail; the tourists don't know the road and tend to drive it too fast on the curves. The tourists weren't familiar with the two-lane road on the trail from Napa to St. Helena.

Joan put breakfast on the table and called Sandy down for breakfast, but she still was concerned; she just had a bad feeling about the bike. As a nurse, she saw more than her share of horrific accidents in the small valley. The winding two-lane highways throughout the valley are often a challenge to the locals and the tourists, and then add the accidents and drownings at Lake Berryessa and the local hospitals are kept busy. As a nurse, Joan saw the results of these accidents every day.

After breakfast, Brad offered to take Sandy for a quick ride on the bike and then to the movies at the small theater downtown. Sandy agreed to the movies but nixed the bike ride. "I don't want to ruin my hair and get grease on my new jeans. But thanks anyway."

Once the kids had left the house, Joan told Bob again that she was really concerned about Brad riding a motorcycle, but Bob just shushed her, reminding her that she was a natural worrier and that he was not worried. He knew his son was a responsible person. Joan turned away as she started the dishes, but she didn't agree with Bob, and the uneasy feeling remained.

Maggie

Over the next few weeks, the women's bocce team continued to win more games than they lost. They were holding third place overall in the A team division. The one or two hours of practice a week were making a big difference in their game. After the game on Thursday night, Maggie suggested a new pizza spot in town for their weekly glass of wine and gabfest, and Maggie could order a pizza or pasta to take home for dinner.

When the women had placed their order, the conversation turned to their husbands and children and their activities. Maggie's son Jeff was good buds with Susie's son Greg. The boys spent a lot of time alternating between the two homes. Both boys were into sports—basketball in the fall and baseball in the spring. They went to the same church camp every summer. Sandy, Joan's daughter, had been close with Lacey, Barb's daughter, when they were younger; but now that Sandy was taking college classes, and Lacey was still a junior in high school, the friendship had cooled a bit. The girls still spoke on the phone and went out occasionally, but were not as tight as they used to be.

Once the women had caught up on the children and their activities, they started the usual discussion and complaints of their spouses. Maggie brought up the subject of Tom and his continued bitching about everything that Maggie did, right or wrong. She said to her friends that Tom either hated her cooking, the way she kept house, and even the way she dressed. She said, "He used to comment on how pretty I am and thought that I looked good even in slacks and a sweater under my white coat at the pharmacy. He was proud of me in my professional life and home life as a wife and mother. Now all he does is put me down. What in the hell is that about?"

Joan told Maggie that he was probably just stressed at work or going through a phase, and half the time her Bob totally ignored her. "He cares more about nuts and bolts and that damn store than my needs. He knows I'm exhausted when I get home from the hospital, and yet he doesn't help around the house." She told Maggie that she wished her Bob was more like Tom, who at least dressed very nice, was always clean shaven, and yes, smelled good. "Bob dresses like a slob and never wears cologne anymore. I buy it for him, but it just sits there. Who can feel romantic for someone that doesn't care about his looks and smells like he rolls in the WD-40 oil he sells?"

The other women just laughed at Joan's colorful description. "By the way, Susie," Barb said, "who was that cute young man that you were speaking with on the other bocce court tonight when you were sitting out the second game? You spent twenty minutes talking to him. Do you know him from somewhere, or is he in the wine business?"

Susie blushed and mentioned that she had met him at a local vintners' meeting a few weeks before, and he was an assistant wine-maker at one of the smaller wineries in the valley. She told them that Jay was very smart and eager to learn the ropes and eventually become the main winemaker for one of the larger wineries. He knew it was a competitive field, and he thought he could learn something from Susie. Susie commented to the others, "Yes, he's cute, but too young for my interests. Although I do find him rather a challenge and interesting to talk to. And wow, he looks good in those tight jeans. I'm just saying, ladies, wow."

Maggie reminded Susie to look but no touching. "He's at least fifteen years younger than you, and you don't want to lead that poor young man astray. Although I wouldn't mind having my own boy toy. Tom is such a pain in the ass sometimes." But speaking of ass, she thought she'd better get her ass home with the linguini and clam pasta she had bought plus the salad and garlic bread she had ordered to go with it. Tom and Jeff will be starving. The other women had placed similar meal orders, and agreed they all needed to get home. They would keep in touch by phone or text until their next bocce practice.

When Maggie got home, she laid out the pasta, salad, and bread and poured a glass of wine for Tom and herself. She called Jeff down to dinner. Tom strolled in, sat down, and told Maggie that it was nice of her to grace them with her presence. Maggie turned to Tom and asked, "What the hell is the matter with you now? I'm not late, I brought home dinner, and you have clean laundry. So get the hell off my back."

Jeff looked at both his parents, picked up his plate, and told them he would finish his dinner in his room while he finished his homework.

Maggie said, "Seriously, Tom, what is the matter? You are always mad at me. I don't know what you want from me anymore. You are making us both miserable, and this isn't good for Jeff either. Jeff and I are going to drive up to Sacramento Saturday to take Michael out to lunch, and I don't want Jeff telling Michael that you and I are having problems. Michael has to keep his mind on his senior year of college and not worry about us. Please tell me, what is the problem? Why are you always angry with me?"

Tom just looked sad and told Maggie that he wasn't sure what the problem was; maybe he was just tired, his practice was growing, and he was thinking of bringing in a new dentist. He had been putting out some inquiries. "I'm sorry," Tom said, "if I've been crabby or distant. I will try to do better. Some days life just seems insurmountable." Maggie decided to take Tom at his word, and she cleaned up the kitchen and went to bed.

Barb

Barb and Jack decided to go to the little town of Rutherford on Friday night for a nice relaxed dinner. Lacey had gone to a school dance with friends, and thirteen-year-old Brenda had offered to stay with eight-year-old Rachel. The girls had plenty of food for dinner and were going to play video games and watch movies. Brenda loved to be in charge and was paid handsomely by her parents. Once Barb and Jack were seated for dinner and had ordered a bottle of Merlot for their dinner, Barb was able to just sit back and relax. The last week at school had been busy with a couple of parent conferences regarding two third-grade boys that had a fistfight in the schoolyard during recess. She told Jack the story of the two boys slugging it out until one of the male teachers had broken the fight up. As a teacher she saw a lot of bad behavior with children, but it always hurt her when the disagreements turned physical.

Once they were halfway through their prime-rib sandwiches, Jack mentioned to Barb that he thought she and the other teacher should have handled the boys fight better. He told her that he'd seen a lot of disputes—physical and otherwise—in the vineyards, and that she should have been harder on the boys and expelled them for at least a week. He then proceeded to tell her that she lacked common sense, and maybe she was not the teacher she thought she was. His voice was getting louder and louder, and the other diners were starting to stare at them.

Barb tried to turn down the temperature by agreeing with Jack, that maybe she could have handled the situation better. She was also silently wondering, had Jack had a few drinks before they went to dinner? He was starting to slur his words, and when he drank more than a few glasses of wine, he got nasty and argumentative. The only thing to do now was to keep calm and try to change the subject. However, Jack was not willing to change the subject, and he continued to berate Barb and make accusations of her not only being a lousy teacher, but also a bad mother and wife.

Barb asked the waiter for the check before things could get more out of hand, and she quickly paid the bill, even though she had not finished her own dinner. She and Jack went out to the car, and she hurried to get to the driver's side before Jack so she could drive them home. Jack, however, pushed her out of the way and jumped into the car and drove off, leaving Barb standing alone in the parking lot.

Now what? Barb did not have enough cash in her purse for a cab, so she just started walking. They were approximately five miles from home, but she had no other options. She just prayed Jack wouldn't have a wreck and kill someone or himself on the way home. She walked close to the wine train tracks so that she was on flatter ground and farther away from the traffic. It took her two hours to get home, and when she arrived home, Jack was sound asleep in their bed.

The girls had already gone to bed, and if they weren't asleep, they didn't seem to be aware that her father had come home without their mother. Barb curled up on the couch with a blanket and cried.

This drunken behavior had happened many times over the last few years. Jack would be good for months at a time, especially after each of the girls had been born, and then for no reason he would just go from fine to not fine, or drunk in a matter of minutes. Barb strongly suspected that Jack hid his stash of wine or booze somewhere in the garage. One or two glasses of wine would not have brought on this bizarre behavior this quickly. Jack was literally two personalities: the nice, caring husband and father and then the mean and cruel monster the next. Barb never knew when this change would occur. She was always walking on eggshells.

She was pretty sure the girls were aware of their Dad's bizarre behavior, but they didn't discuss it, and she was hesitant to bring it up. Barb had many times considered leaving Jack and moving into a small rental house with the girls, but as a teacher, she made less money than Jack and she wasn't sure that she could financially swing it. She just kept praying for better times and Jack to come to his senses.

The next morning, before the girls came down for breakfast, Jack asked Barb why she had chosen to walk home and what was wrong with her. He didn't remember his nasty comments or the fact that he had started the fight and driven off leaving Barb standing in the dark parking lot. Jack did say he was sorry, but he still felt that Barb had made the choice to walk home. And if she had agreed that she could have handled the school situation better, the fight would never had started in the first place. So basically, it was still Barb's fault. Jack quickly forgot the whole episode and brushed Barb's concerns under the rug.

CHAPTER 8

Susie

On Thursday night at bocce, during the third game, Susie wasn't playing so she wandered over to the next court to chat with Jay again. Jay was glad to see her and told Susie how pretty she looked. "Well, thank you, kind sir. You look pretty good yourself," Susie teased back.

Jay asked what she was doing after the game tonight. "Would you like to go out for a drink or a cup of coffee when we are finished?"

Susie told him that she had another commitment for that night, but maybe another night. Jay then suggested Monday night at six or seven. at one of the local wine bars. Susie thought about it for a minute and thought, *Why not? What can one little drink hurt? He just wants my advice on wine making. It's all business.*

"Okay, why not? Let's make it six." Susie named the wine bar that they would meet at. Then she wandered back to her team as they won the third game.

When the four friends arrived at the wine bar for their weekly gabfest and glass of wine, Barb told Susie that she had noticed her chatting with that cute young guy again and asked what was going on. Susie told Barb and the others that Jay was just seeking professional advice, and she had agreed to meet him for a drink on Monday night, just to be sociable. Maggie told Susie that she thought she was playing with fire, and she thought she should not meet with Jay, but maybe offer advice through e-mails and texts. Maggie said, "It may be perfectly harmless, but it just doesn't look good."

Joan agreed. "What will your husband think? I don't think Mark would like it."

But Susie, interrupted Joan. "Oh my gosh, Mark is always in the city on Monday nights, and he wouldn't care anyway. He doesn't pay the slightest bit of attention to me anyway. It's kind of nice to have a cute guy think I'm fun and maybe even pretty." Susie went on to change the subject and asked how the other three women were doing.

They changed the subject to who was going to host the next month's dinner party, and it was decided that Maggie and Tom would host it. Tom and Mark got along well together, and they could play cards after dinner. The four couples enjoyed bridge and canasta. Bob and Jack had more in common and enjoyed fishing and duck hunting; overall, the couples enjoyed each other's company.

Susie got home and made grilled-cheese sandwiches and soup for her and Greg. Mark was staying in the city again tonight after a late-night meeting. He had a pullout couch and bathroom in his San Francisco office, so he could easily stay over. Mark's being gone that night gave Susie more time to think and wonder if she had made a mistake agreeing to meet with Jay on Monday night. But in the end, she convinced herself that it was just harmless; he was new to the valley and needed a friend in the business. No big deal.

Saturday, Mark played golf with Tom, and Susie took Greg downtown to buy new running shoes and pick up a few new shirts. Saturday night, Greg was going to hang out with his buddies, and Susie suggested that she and Mark go out for a quiet dinner. Susie was always hopeful that Mark would start to be a more attentive father and husband.

Susie found Mark agreeable for a night out, and they had a very pleasant dinner at one of the nicer restaurants in St. Helena. Toward the end of dinner, Susie brought up the subject of Greg. She told Mark that she was concerned about Greg's behavior: she thought he was getting thinner and seemed more on edge, and he was spending more and more time out with friends and was receiving a lot of phone calls from boys that she had never met or heard of. She asked Mark, "Do you think something is going on? His grades slipped again last semester, and I'm afraid he may be hanging with a bad crowd. And if his grades stay the way they are, he won't get into a good college."

Mark just laughed off Susie's concerns about Greg and told her he was a good kid. And with his busy schedule with sports and friends, it was normal to have his grades fluctuate. Mark repeated, "Susie, you worry too much. Greg's fine. He's just like his dad—a popular kid. Just lay off him, he'll be fine."

Susie agreed to back off and just remind Greg to stay focused on his homework, but she wouldn't push or interrogate him. They drove home, and this time, Mark did make a half-hearted attempt to make love with Susie once they went to bed. Susie felt that Mark was responding more out of obligation than passion. It was something that they both felt was their duty once a month or so.

Wow, Susie thought, *that was boring*. And in her mind she was picturing what sex would be like with Jay. On his side of the bed, Mark was thinking the same thing, less than exciting, and visualizing his secretary, Kim, a very curvy young woman. Kim was very attentive to Mark and always seemed to brush up against him whenever she came close to his desk. Kim was maybe twenty-five and had worked for him for the last six months. She had replaced Mary, his sixty-two-year-old secretary that had retired. He had to admit that Kim maybe wasn't as professional as Mary, but she was a hell of a lot better to look at. Kim's interest made him feel young and desired again.

Susie met with Jay on Monday night at the agreed time and wine bar. The conversation started out professional and then turned more casual. Susie told Jay the story of her becoming of one of the best winemakers in the valley and her upward struggle in such a man's field. It had taken her years to get to the point of the senior winemaker, and she had suffered many putdowns, off-color remarks, and groping through the years. She told him she hadn't dared complain about the flirting and inappropriate behavior, but she had tried to just laugh it off and keep out of harm's way. She wore looser blouses and jeans and wore no makeup at work. It's a man's world, and if you claim sexual harassment, you get fired or called a tease or bitch. Better to keep your mouth shut.

Jay was very comforting and apologetic for the hassle she had received; he was a younger and more understanding male and had seen the unfairness in the workplace for women. Jay made Susie feel justified and vindicated. It felt good to be appreciated for once.

The evening went well, and when Jay suggested they meet again the next Monday night to just go over a few questions that he had regarding a new process involving the drip system for grapes and the best grapes to plant in certain areas, Susie quickly agreed. She just wanted to be helpful to this kind young man.

CHAPTER 9

Joan

When Joan went to work on Monday morning, she was called into the administrator's office as soon as she arrived on the ward. *Oh great*, she thought, *now what?* There was a nice-looking man standing next to the administrator. He was introduced to Joan as Dr. Frank Harris, a new cardiologist at the hospital.

Dr. Harris had just transferred here from Chicago. Dr. Hart, the administrator, asked Joan to please show Dr. Harris around the hospital and introduce him to the staff. Joan had worked at the hospital for years and was well respected among the doctors and nurses.

Of course, Joan would be glad to give Dr. Harris the tour. They spent the next two hours hitting all the various wards: OB, Neurology, Pediatrics, Surgery, the Emergency Rooms, and others. Dr. Harris was very impressed and told Joan that he had come from a much-larger hospital in Chicago, and he was charmed with this small and efficient hospital in the valley. He had heard about the Napa Valley of course but had never visited and was anxious to try the famous restaurants and excellent wines.

After the tour Joan and Dr. Harris went to the cafeteria for a quick lunch. Joan asked Dr. Harris why would he leave a big hospital in Chicago to come to such a small hospital in the valley. Dr. Harris looked sad for a moment, and then explained that his wife had died fourteen months ago of breast cancer, and he needed a fresh start. He and his wife had never been able to have children, and he just needed to get away from the memories. She had died in the hospital he was on staff at, and he just couldn't face the ghosts anymore.

Joan told him she totally understood, and she was glad to welcome him to the valley. Dr. Harris asked Joan to please call him Frank, and would it be okay if he called her Joan? Absolutely, Joan agreed. Joan thought, how sad, Dr. Harris was a good-looking man with slightly graying hair, maybe fifty-five years old or so. Too young to lose his wife.

After lunch, Joan went back to her ward, and Dr. Harris—Frank—went back to the administrator's office to go over his schedule and hours. Dr. Harris commented to Dr. Hart, "How sweet and kind Joan had been" as he thought to himself, *And a very pretty lady too.*

That night at dinner, Joan told Bob and Sandy about the new doctor from Chicago and what a sad story his life had been. Bob responded, "Yeah it's a shame, but he'll get over it. And with the money he makes, and being a doctor, the single women in this valley will be all over him. He won't be lonely for long."

Sandy responded, "Dad, I don't think that's very kind. I'm sure this man is suffering, and not all men jump right back in the saddle. Men need time to grieve too."

Joan agreed, "He seems to be genuinely heartbroken, and I really like him. He has a great reputation of not only being a good doctor, but also an empathic human being. That's a winning score in my book."

When Bob frowned, Joan wondered if Bob was still upset about not finishing college and law school and was maybe a little jealous of Dr. Harris, who had accomplished everything Bob had not.

On Friday, Frank—Dr. Harris—asked Joan to have lunch with him again. He told her he was looking for a rental house and was wondering if she had time on either Saturday or Sunday to go with him to look at a couple of possibilities, since she knew the area so well. She agreed that she did have time on Sunday morning and would meet him at the coffee shop on Main Street, and she would bring a map.

Friday night at dinner, Joan told Bob that she was going to take Dr. Harris to look at rental property on Sunday morning at ten, and she would go to early mass, so that she would have time to help Dr. Harris. Bob told her he didn't care one way or another, and he was going fishing with some friend and wouldn't be home until early evening. He heard the bass were really running at the lake. He did tell Joan, though, "Don't get too involved with this doctor. He will expect you to start doing his laundry and cooking his meals. Let him hire a housekeeper."

"Right, Bob, I'm sure that Dr. Harris wants me to take in his laundry. I will be sure to make sure and ask him if he likes starch in his shirts. Sometimes I don't believe the way you think."

Bob just laughed. "Just make sure you don't starch his shorts."

Maggie

Saturday morning, as Maggie was finishing up the breakfast dishes, she asked Jeff if he was going to go to the harvest dance at the high school that evening. She told Jeff that she had seen a poster for the dance at the local coffee shop, and since he hadn't mentioned it, she was wondering if he was going.

Jeff had gotten his driver's license in the last month and had been driving Maggie's car whenever she wasn't using it. They were going to take Jeff used-car shopping in the next few months, but they wanted him to get a few more miles under his belt before they did. "So, Jeff," Maggie asked, "are you going to the dance? And who did you invite? I can order a corsage at the florist. It's not too late."

Jeff looked down at his feet and answered, "No, Mom, I'm just going to hang with the guys. I think we're going to play basketball at Ed's house tonight and then order pizza. Is it all right if I stay over at Ed's after dinner?"

Maggie told Jeff that that was fine, but she wondered why he wasn't interested. He had always liked to dance, but she hadn't seen him with any girls for quite a while. He had always gone to dances with Carrie, their neighbor girl, and the two kids had been friends for years. She was curious if Jeff and Carrie had a falling out. She would ask Carrie's mom when she got a chance. Jeff went back up to his room to finish his homework before he left for his friend's house.

In the afternoon when Tom got home from playing golf, Maggie mentioned to Tom her concerns about Jeff not wanting to go to the dance. "Do you think he and Carrie had a fight or if he has other problems? I haven't heard him mention a girl he likes in months."

Tom gave her a frosty look and told her that she was nuts, and Jeff just hadn't found a girl he liked yet. "The kid's a man's man like his dad, and he's discerning. He's picky. He wants only the best."

Maggie tended to agree with Tom. "You're right, I'm just worrying over nothing. I just want Jeff to be happy. It just seems harder to be a teenager now than we were teenagers. With social media, there is so much bullying and unkindness with these kids. We didn't have this problem with Michael. Michael was popular and into sports and girls. There were always tons of his friends around our house. And now Jeff keeps to himself, and he never brings friends home anymore, just Greg occasionally."

Tom once again reiterated, "Maggie, just leave the kid alone. He knows what he's doing. He's maintaining good grades, and if he's not as social as you are, so be it. You're social enough for the entire family." Tom then went upstairs to change into some work clothes and mow the lawn.

Maggie decided to call Michael at his dorm and get his thoughts on Jeff. The boys had always been close, even though there was a six-year age gap. Michael answered his cell, "Yeah, Mom, what's going on? Is everyone okay? Is someone sick?"

Maggie assured Michael that they were all fine. She told Michael that she was a little concerned about Jeff and his lack of social interaction, especially with girls. She wanted Michael's thoughts on this. Maybe Jeff had talked to Michael instead of confiding in his parents.

Michael told his mom, "I think Jeff's fine. He's always been a quiet kid, more introspective than I am. And he keeps his own council. I can come home next weekend and talk to Jeff if that would make you feel better, and I'll bring my dirty laundry. How does that sound? And maybe you could make my favorite pumpkin cake or even a devil's food cake would work. Okay, does that reassure you a bit?"

Maggie just laughed and told Michael how impressed she was with his new big college words, introspective, curious, and really, maybe he was learning something in college. "I'm glad our money is going to good use for school and just not for partying and girls." She asked Michael if he had declared his major, and would he be going to apply to dental school? Or maybe go for his MBA? She smiled and said, "You know your dad and I just want you to follow your dream. If you want to be a dentist and join Dad in his practice, he would love it. But we just want the best for you, and whatever you decide on will make us happy. We have always been so proud of you."

Michael said, "Hey, Mom, I've got to go. I'm playing ball with the guys this afternoon, but I promise to come home next weekend and talk to the little twerp. Not sure he'll break down and spill his guts to me, but I'll give him the usual pep talk that you always gave me. Love you, Mom, gotta go."

Maggie always felt better after talking to her oldest son. Michael had always been the crazy prankster when he was a teenager, and he had given both his parents their share of worry during those crazy years. He had excelled in basketball and football, while barely scraping by with a B average. He had partied every weekend, snuck liquor bottles out of the house, and filled the remaining bottles with water. He had tried smoking pot and missed every curfew his parents had set. He was a good-looking boy, six two, green eyed like his dad, and was a chic magnet. Tom had given Michael the talk early and made sure he was provided with condoms and sobering information about pregnancy and responsibility. Michael had always laughed off their concerns, telling them that he knew the score and wasn't stupid enough to become a father at seventeen. He had borrowed his mom's car more than once in the middle of the night without permission even before he had a license. He had been a teenage terror and yet always managed to make his parents smile with his crazy antics and pranks. Graduation seemed to be the turning point, and Michael was eager to head off to college, and his parents were praying that Michael would turn out to be a responsible adult. So far, so good—his grades were holding. And even if he did still party too much, he was on schedule to graduate the next June.

Maggie had to smile to herself; she had raised two good boys, just very different in personality and looks. But she was extremely proud of both boys. *Jeff will be okay, his big brother will find out if something is bothering him, and I am just being a mom, worrying when there is nothing to worry about.*

Barb

Barb got home from school at four after staying late to grade papers, and she found Brenda and Rachel at the kitchen table doing their homework. Barb asked the girls, "Where is your sister Lacey? She should have been home by now. Did you see her after school? Did she walk home with you?"

"No, Mom," Brenda told her. "I walked over to the Rachel's school to walk home with her, but I haven't seen Lacey since this morning. Maybe she stayed late to finish a project. I know she's been having a problem with biology and wanted to talk to her teacher about taking on some extra credit work. I'm sure she's fine. Don't worry, Mom, Lacey's a big girl. She'll be home any minute."

An hour later, Lacey ran through the front door and went straight to her room without saying a word to her mom or sisters. She locked the door and threw herself down on the bed and burst into tears. Barb ran up the stairs and knocked on Lacey's door. "Honey, are you okay? What's wrong? Can I come in and talk to you?"

Lacey yelled back through the closed door, "I'm fine, Mom! I just don't feel like talking. I just need to work on my biology home-work. Please just give me some space." Barb called out to Lacey one more time, and when she got no response, she went back downstairs. Barb was perplexed; Lacey never behaved this way. She was always a sunny, happy teenager. What the hell happened to make her so upset? Had she had a fight with the nice guy, Ty, that Lacey had been seeing for the last two months? *That must be it*, she thought, *maybe they had a little fight. I'll give her some space. I'm sure she'll talk to me when she's ready.*

Lacey just lay on her bed and kept going over the whole ugly picture in her mind. Had she done something to Mr. Martin to make him act like that? She had always been polite and respectful to him. And all she had done was stay after class to ask Mr. Martin if he could assign her an extra-credit project to bring up her grade. Biology was giving her some problems, and her grade had slipped down to a C. When she had asked Mr. Martin if he could give her some extra-credit work, he had responded with "What will you do for me if I help you out?" He then put his hand on her breast and pulled her close to him. "Do you understand what I'm saying?" He then put his hand up her short skirt and reached into her panties. "I think you understand what I want. You help me, and I help you." As he spoke, he unzipped his pants and put her hand on his genitals.

Lacey, pulled back, shocked. "Please, Mr. Martin, I don't understand. I don't want to do this. Why are you doing this?"

Mr. Martin told Lacey, "You walk in here with tight blouses and short skirts and flaunt yourself in front of all the boys in the class. You look like the slut that you are, so don't play innocent with me. I'm sure you're putting out for Ty and some of the other boys. Come on, share the wealth. If you don't play along with me, I will see that you mother gets fired from her teaching position. The principal at your mom's school is my cousin, and I can just put a little bug in her ear, and your mom is history. If you tell anyone about this little conversation, I will see your mom is fired immediately. I can ruin your family, so you'd better think about cooperating. I will expect you to be in a better mood, say, next Monday afternoon at four in my classroom. Do you get my drift, Lacey?"

Lacey had just turned and ran out of the classroom and all the way home. She knew she couldn't tell anyone. Her mother would be furious, fight back with Mr. Martin, and would be fired. Her father would go nuts; when he drank too much, which he did frequently, he could get really nasty. What if her father killed Mr. Martin? Or even if he beat him up? Their family would be humiliated and ruined.

She had to think about what she should do. What if she wore baggy clothes and no makeup? If she looked less attractive, maybe Mr. Martin would lose interest. She didn't think she dressed like a slut; she dressed like all the other girls her age. Yes, Lacey thought, she was large busted, but that wasn't her fault. Her mother had never told her to dress differently, or complained about her clothes. Lacey decided that was all she could do—make herself look less attractive. Maybe she could make Mr. Martin think she was crazy, then he would leave her alone. She had read about teenagers who would cut themselves to make the inner pain go away. What if she started cutting herself and let Mr. Martin see the scars? Maybe he would think she was crazy? She went into her dad's bathroom and pulled a razor out of this cabinet and took it into her bedroom. *Maybe*, she thought, *just a little cut on my arm, and then my thigh, and if Mr. Martin sees it, he'll think I'm crazy.* Lacey made a small cut on her arm, and when it didn't bleed, she cut a deeper gash in her thigh until this cut did bleed.

Wow, she thought, *maybe this is not such a bad idea. It hurts, but it also feels like I'm fighting back in my own way. This is something I can control and Mr. Martin can't. I can choose to cut or not, I can choose to eat or not. I still have some control over my own body. I will not let Mr. Martin destroy my family.*

Downstairs, Barb was helping Rachel with her homework. Barb was worried about Lacey, but she remembered how emotional she had been in those teenage years, and assumed that Lacey was going through the same angst. Barb would talk to Jack about it tonight when he got home. Hopefully, he would stay sober enough to have a serious conversation with her. She knew Jack loved all of his daughters and would do anything to keep them safe.

Susie

Susie and Jay met again at the same little wine bar on Monday night. Susie was getting more comfortable with Jay and really enjoyed his company. After each ordered a good glass of pinot, Jay reached over and touched Susie's hand and told her how much he appreciated her input and the knowledge she was sharing with him. Susie told him that it was nice to spend time with a man that actually listened to her and thought she had a brain in her head. She told Jay that her husband Mark never listened to her, and she felt unappreciated at home. Susie complained that when Mark was home his mind was elsewhere, and she felt diminished as a woman and a person. "Sorry, Jay, I don't mean to bring my personal problems to you. I should not have mentioned it."

Jay leaned over and put his arm around Susie, and he told her that he thought she was a beautiful and an intelligent woman, and her husband was a fool to not appreciate her. "The guy must be an idiot not to cherish what he has. Any other man would be beating down the door to get to you, including me."

Susie laughed and said, "Well, thank you, kind sir. From your lips to Mark's ears. That is very kind of you to say about a woman old enough to be your mother. Well, maybe your older sister. I may not believe you, but it's nice to hear anyway. Sometimes I feel old and useless like a dried-up old sponge."

Now Jay laughed. "Honey, you are anything but old. And if anything, you are underused. You just need a real man to throw out the sponge and bring out the real woman hiding her assets. I don't mean to be forward, and I don't want to embarrass you, but I find you to be a beautiful desirable woman. And I would like to get to know you better, if I may be so forward."

Wow, Susie wasn't sure what to think, but she was certainly flattered to hear such kind works from this very good-looking young man. Yes, Susie did find Jay very attractive and desirable, but she wasn't ready to get involved in an affair with a much younger man, or was she? Why didn't Mark think she was attractive and desirable anymore? Why didn't he say the beautiful words to her that Jay did? Maybe Mark didn't love her anymore; why had they grown so far apart?

Jay looked into Susie's eyes, and asked her, "So what do you think? Can we still see each other once a while? We can keep it professional or at least remain just friends. Or we can take it to the next level, I'm good with either. It's obvious that I would like to get to know you a lot better, and I will let you set the rules. But I am also not going to let you out of my life now that I've found you."

Susie told Jay, "Okay, for now let's just be friends. But yes, I would like to continue to see you. You are great for my ego if nothing else, and I like to talk you about the changes in the wine industry." They agreed to meet again next Monday at the same wine bar.

When Susie got home, she wasn't surprised that Mark wasn't home, and Greg told her that his dad had called and told him that he had a late meeting and would be staying the night in the city. Greg told his mom that he had made a grilled-cheese sandwich for dinner and was going upstairs to do his homework. Susie decided to have a yogurt for dinner and head to upstairs herself; she had a lot to think about.

When Mark had called home to tell Greg he was staying in the city, he hadn't mentioned to Greg that he was having dinner with Kim his secretary, and the late meeting had been cancelled. Kim was certainly more interesting to talk to than Susie, and she was 100 percent prettier than Susie. Or maybe it was just because she was younger and dressed more seductively. Mark felt younger and more energetic when he was with Kim. He knew than Kim looked up to him the way Susie used to and no longer did. When had his relationship with his wife become so boring?

CHAPTER 13

Joan

On Friday night, Joan and Sandy had decided to go out to dinner and then a movie together since Bob had late hours at the store on two Friday nights a month. Sandy was without a date for the night and was glad to spend time with her mom. They had chosen one of the small Mexican restaurants that was so good on Main Street.

After they had ordered dinner, Joan asked Sandy about school, and Sandy responded that she was enjoying her classes but that chemistry was hard as hell. To complete nursing school it was a required course, so she had to suck it up, but she told her mom that the class still sucked. Joan laughed and told Sandy that she had barely squeaked by with chemistry herself; otherwise, she would be glad to help.

Joan said to Sandy, "I have something to ask you. Barb is concerned about Lacey and how withdrawn Lacey has been the last week or two. Lacey goes to school, comes home, and locks herself in her room. She has started dressing like a street bum in sweats and no makeup. Joan is really worried about her. Have you spoken to her at all lately?"

Sandy told her mom that she hadn't spoken to her in weeks, but she would be glad to invite Lacey to breakfast on Sunday morning and see if she could find out what was bothering Lacey. Sandy laughed and said, "She probably is having guy problems, and that can put any girl in the frumps. But she doesn't need to go overboard and dress like a bum and give up makeup. Some things like makeup are just too important to give up. You know I never leave the house after eight. without eye makeup. I don't want to scare to locals."

Joan reached over and gave Sandy a hug. "That's what I love about my girl, her modesty and sensible attitude. You're going to make a great nurse, and I can't wait until you can work at the hospital with your old mom."

The women had a pleasant evening, and as they left the restaurant, Sandy promised to give Lacey a call for Sunday morning. Sandy had a date Saturday night but would fit Lacey in between studying for the chemistry test.

Sandy was as good as her word and called Lacey on Saturday morning and invited her to the local diner for Sunday-morning brunch. At first Lacey declined, but Sandy pushed and told her she wouldn't take no for an answer, and that Lacey would be doing Sandy a favor. Lacey finally agreed to meet Sandy at the diner at ten.

Sunday morning, Sandy was already seated when Lacey walked in and sat down at the table. Joan had been right: Lacey looked like a homeless woman, baggy clothes, no makeup, and her hair looked matted and greasy. Normally, Lacey was always well dressed and groomed, so this change was dramatic. Sandy smiled and said to Lacey, "Is something going on with you since you look like a bag lady without the bag? I love you dearly, girl, but you are an embarrassment to be seen with. Are you having boyfriend problems or trouble at home?"

Lacey looked down at the menu with tears in her eyes and said, "No, I'm fine, just getting a little overwhelmed with homework. The junior year is tough, and I need to get into a good college. Let's order waffles with bacon, and let's talk about something more pleasant."

Sandy was certainly not convinced that all this change in Lacey was being caused by homework, but she thought she would let it ride for a bit and have a pleasant breakfast. They both placed their order, and then Sandy changed the subject to talk about her college classes and the guy that she was dating. She was going to keep the subject light, and maybe Lacey would open up.

Once they had started eating, Sandy noticed Lacey push up her sleeves, and Sandy saw an ugly red scar on Lacey's forearm. Sandy said, "Oh my gosh, Lacey, what happened to your arm?"

Lacey just shrugged it off, and told her that she had cut her arm washing dishes and broken a glass. Lacey continued it was no big deal, but she looked uncomfortable, even embarrassed.

Sandy had the uneasy feeling that something serious was going on with Lacey, and she was going to get to the bottom of it. Lacey was like a younger sister to Sandy, and she felt a responsibility to Lacey. Sandy decided that she was going to keep a closer eye on Lacey and just pop in on her now and then.

Meanwhile, on Sunday morning, Joan was taking Dr. Frank Harris house hunting. After seeing four possible rentals, they found a cute two-bedroom cottage on Spring St. It had a charming, updated kitchen and a warm living room with a stone fireplace. The rent was reasonable and had an option to buy if Dr. Harris decided to stay on in St. Helena. Frank told Joan that he loved it and it felt homey, and the second bedroom could be used as an office. After signing the rental agreement with the agent, Frank asked Joan if he could take her to lunch as a reward for helping him in his search.

Joan agreed and mentioned the name of a sweet little restaurant on one of the side streets off Main. She told Frank that they served a great frittata as well as other delicious items, and she loved their salads. Frank told her that sounded perfect, and he offered to drive her back to her car later.

Once seated, Frank insisted on ordering a bottle of champagne to celebrate his finding his perfect new home. He patted Joan's hand and told her, "I couldn't have done it without you. I truly believe you bring me good luck." Lunch was as delicious as Joan had promised, and Frank and Joan continued to chat about their work, her children, and his busy schedule at the hospital.

When Frank drove Joan back to her car after lunch, he shyly asked if maybe they could get together for lunch once in a while. He really would like to have a friend in his new town. Joan told Frank that she would enjoy that. "You can't have too many friends, and I would honored to be counted as one."

When Joan drove home, she thought of what a nice time she had with Frank. He was a kind man, easy to talk to, and the fact that he was a good-looking man didn't hurt either. She was looking forward to seeing him at the hospital, and maybe at lunch again too. After all, she thought, what's the harm?

CHAPTER 14

Barb

Barb and Jack had been invited to have dinner at a local restaurant with one of Bob's new coworkers and his wife. Barb was anxious to meet the new couple and was glad that Jack was making friends. The restaurant had just been opened a few months but had received great reviews. Barb spent a little extra time with her makeup and put on a new dress. She aimed to impress and wanted Jack to be proud of her. Barb always tried to appease Jack and to never give him a reason to complain.

When Jack and Barb arrived at the restaurant, Fred and his wife Nancy were already seated and waiting for Jack and Barb. Fred had ordered a nice bottle of Merlot and four glasses while they were waiting. Jack introduced his wife to Fred and Nancy as Fred poured the wine, and Fred thanked Jack for joining him and his wife for dinner. Fred told Barb that everyone in St. Helena had been so warm and welcoming. And they felt very comfortable in their rental house, and their two sons, seven and nine, were enjoying their new school.

The couples ordered dinner and were enjoying the music that a trio was playing in the corner of the room. On weekends the restaurant would host different music groups. The music was just light jazz and very pleasant. Over the second glass of wine, Jack suddenly seemed to notice the music, and he called the hostess over and asked that they please stop the music—he was finding it annoying.

The hostess explained that the other patrons were enjoying the music, and the trio had been hired to play that night until ten. When the hostess seemed unwilling to follow Jack's orders, Jack demanded to see the restaurant manager. The manager was summoned to the table, and Jack again explained that he found the music annoying and offensive and demanded that the music be stopped. As the manager continued to explain that the other guests were enjoying the music, Jack raised his voice and told the manager that he would insist that the music be stopped, or he and his wife would leave the premises.

Barb was so embarrassed and tried to calm Jack down, telling him and the manager that she was enjoying the music, and pleaded with Jack to behave and think of the other guests. By this time Jack's face was getting redder and his voice louder with his demands. Fred and Nancy looked very uncomfortable and continued to stare down at their laps.

The manager walked away just as the plates of food were served. Jack continued to mutter about the terrible service until the manager walked back over to the table and grabbed Barb and Jack's full plates and told Barb to get Jack the hell out of her restaurant. Jack told her, "Gladly," and threw down his napkin and walked out of the restaurant. Barb apologized to the manager and the other couple, and she tried to give a credit card to the manager, but the manager told her, "Just send me a check. I don't want to deal with your husband a minute longer than necessary."

Totally humiliated and with tears in her eyes, Barb followed Jack out of the restaurant. When Barb got to the parking lot, Jack was driving off, leaving Barb stranded in the parking lot. With no other options, Barb began the twenty-minute walk home. She couldn't go back in the restaurant, and she was too embarrassed to ask Fred and Nancy for a ride home, so she just began the long walk home.

When Barb arrived home, Jack was already in bed sound asleep. Barb checked on the girls: Rachel and Brenda were watching TV, and Lacey had locked herself in her bedroom. The girls asked Barb why they were home so early, and Barb told them that their dad wasn't feeling well, and he came home early. Barb said she had chosen to walk since it was such a nice night.

Neither girl believed Barb. They had seen their father stagger in, but they didn't want to hurt their mother, so they just went along with the lie and agreed that it had been a beautiful night. Barb stayed in the kitchen finding things to do until the girls went to bed, and then she would make up a bed for herself on the couch. There was no way she was going to share a bed with Jack. My god, she thought, how much more could she take?

The next morning, when Jack came down to breakfast, Jack asked Barb why she had slept on the couch. Barb told him to keep his voice down; she didn't want the girls to know that she had slept on the couch or that they were having problems. Jack asked, "What problems? What are you talking about?"

Barb said, "Don't you remember last night? We were kicked out of the restaurant, leaving your friends to dine alone, and it was rude. I wouldn't be surprised if they never speak to you again. And on top of that, you drove off and left me to walk home alone. You could have gotten a DUI, and we sure as hell can't afford that. I suggest you get your ass on the phone and apologize to Fred and Nancy. You need to get you're drinking under control, or I'm taking the girls and leaving."

Jack gave Barb a hug and told her how sorry he was and that he would call up Fred right now and apologize. He would just say that he hadn't had lunch, and the wine went to his head. He would tell them that he knew he had been a jerk, and it wouldn't happen again.

"I know this, Barb. You'll never leave me. You know you couldn't make it on a teacher's salary, and you know you love me, mistakes and all. Sometimes I drink a little too much, and I will try to do better." Jack then left the kitchen to call Fred and make up a story and apologize. He knew Fred would understand; guys always stick together, and after all it was no big deal.

Barb just sagged into the nearest chair, thinking how long could she put up with this. When Jack was sober, he was a nice guy and a good dad, but when he was drinking, he was unbearable to be around

And unpredictable. She never knew what he would do next. What if he got a DUI or, worse, killed someone? Then how would she feel? She had never spoken her fears to her friends. She didn't want them to think less of her, or hate Jack, but she knew she needed a friend to talk out her worse fears. *Maybe the next time the four of us get together, maybe I'll bring up at least some of it. We'll see. I'll think about it.*

And then she went to find her daughters and see if they wanted to see a movie or go bowling.

CHAPTER 15

Maggie

Maggie was thrilled on Saturday morning when Michael walked into the house with a garbage bag full of dirty laundry. She gave Michael a hug, and told him, "I missed you, and I am so glad to see you even with your dirty laundry. Tell me all about school, girls, your friends, everything. I want to hear it all. Boy do we miss you around the house."

Michael laughed and said, "Slow down, Mom. I will tell you everything, or at least what's reasonable for your ears, some things are censored. I'm going to take Jeff to lunch and see what makes him tick. Or in your language, what's bothering him. I'm sure you're just overreacting, like you normally do. But I will put the kid under the hot lights and interrogate him."

Maggie agreed and told Michael that she would behave, but she expected to get all the dirt tonight at dinner. She would make his favorite meal, and they would have plenty of time to catch up. She told Michael that Jeff had been excited to see his big brother, and he was waiting upstairs doing his homework. "Just go on up or holler like you always do." She told him she actually missed his booming voice, slamming doors as he raced in and out to join friends, and the glass rings that he always left on the tabletops. She gave Michael another hug and said, "I must be losing my mind to say this, but I like your longer hair, and I do believe you're getting cuter—excuse me—more handsome every day. The girls must think you're hot. That is the expression, right?"

"You're right, Mom, I'm totally hot." And then Michael ran up the stairs to find Jeff and take him out for pizza. Jeff had been waiting for Michael and had been playing video games until his big brother arrived. He had finished his homework last night but hadn't told his mother. He didn't want her to think he was lame, and he really didn't want to get into a discussion with his mom, so he just claimed he had homework.

Michael burst into Jeff's room and gave his brother a hug and said, "Let's go, squirt, I'm buying lunch. Well, maybe Mom is buying since I have the credit card she gave me. So basically, I'm buying." Jeff laughed and thought how much he really missed his big brother. Michael had always had Jeff's back. When Michael was home, nobody teased or bullied Jeff, but things had certainly changed since then.

Both boys decided on a small pizza parlor that they had eaten at for years. The food was good, and it was quiet enough to talk without being overheard. Once they had ordered a pizza and a Coke for Jeff and a beer for Michael, they found a table, and Michael got right to the point.

Michael looked at Jeff and said, "Okay, kid, what's going on? Mom said you didn't want to go to the dance. You're spending more time alone. What's the deal? Is someone at school giving you a hard time? Is it a girl that you like and she's not interested? It can't be the schoolwork. You've always been brainier than me. So you can tell me, and I promise not to share with Mom or Dad. Your secret is safe with me."

Jeff's eyes started to tear up, and he looked uncomfortable, as he said to Michael, "I think something is wrong with me. Like maybe I like boys, or I'm gay or something. I'm not sure, but pretty sure that I'm weird. I thought I liked girls, and I like to kiss them, but I don't want to do more than that. I haven't kissed or done anything with guys either, but I feel an attraction when I'm around certain guys. You know that warm, fluttery feeling in the pit of your stomach? I think some of the guys suspect that I'm weird, and I'm getting teased at school by a couple of guys on the football team. Dirty words have been written on my gym locker, and some of the girls have laughed at me. I don't know what to do. I hate going to school. Maybe I'll drop out or transfer to another school."

"Wow," Michael said, "you've been carrying a heavy load around by yourself. First off, don't quit school. That's just plain stupid. As far as the guys teasing or bullying you, the best thing to do is just ignore them or laugh it off. If they know it doesn't bother you, they'll stop. Now they know it gets to you, so they keep it up. I also think you need to share this with Mom and Dad. Both are understanding professionals in the medical field, and they won't be shocked if you are gay, and they will support and love you. If you are gay, you didn't invent it, and you won't be the first person, guy or girl, to be gay. So get over yourself. I do, however, want you to be careful. If you decide to experiment with a guy or girl, use condoms and common sense."

Jeff felt better after sharing his feelings with Michael. And the fact that Michael had not been shocked or disgusted made Jeff feel better about himself. He told Michael that he would think about telling his parents, but he didn't want to do it yet. He still wanted to think about it, since he wasn't really sure himself yet. He was hoping for a miracle, that he would wake up one morning and be straight. In his heart he knew this wasn't going to happen, but his head was still hoping.

The boys went on to talk about sports and other subjects, and lunch was enjoyable for both. Jeff had to admit to himself how much he missed having his older brother at home. Michael had always had Jeff's back. Maybe Jeff and Michael could go camping together this summer, just the two of them, like they used to when they were kids. Tent camping, sleeping under the stars, cooking over a camp stove. Maybe they could go to Lake Tahoe for a week. Jeff mentioned these thoughts, and Michael agreed that he would love to go to Tahoe for a week in July. Michael laughed and said, "I could visit the casinos once I tuck you into your sleeping bag at night, or I think some of the casinos have game rooms for kids. We'll check it out."

The family had a good dinner that night with Tom even getting involved in the conversations, especially when sports were brought up. Tom had always been proud of Michael's sports ability and wished that Jeff was more like his brother in that area. Jeff was decent at sports, but Michael had been a star, with every girl in high school vying to wear Michael's letterman jacket. Michael had changed girlfriends more than most guys change their socks.

Maggie was just thrilled to have her family together again for one weekend. She noticed that Jeff seemed more relaxed now that his brother was home. Maybe the boys had talked things out, and Jeff was feeling more confident. Maggie was pretty sure that Jeff was having girl problems, and Michael had offered some guy advice. She would be sad to see Michael leave the next morning, but they kept in touch through e-mail and texts. Overall, it had been a good weekend, and she felt reassured that both boys were in a good place in their lives.

CHAPTER 16

Susie

Susie was rushing out of the house on Monday night to meet Jay at the wine bar, when Greg walked into the house and started giggling as he tripped over the cat. Susie asked Greg where he had been; she had thought he would have been home from school several hours ago. Greg just laughed and told his mom that he had been hanging out with the guys after school. He told Susie, "Hey, we were just tossing a few basketballs around. No biggie, Mom, no laws broken. I'm going upstairs to do my homework. I'm not hungry, but if I want something, I'll make a sandwich."

"Susie told Greg that she was going out for a couple of hours, and Dad would be staying in the city tonight. But if you need me, just call my cell phone. Hey, just a thought, why don't you invite Jeff over to have dinner with you or watch a movie? I haven't seen Jeff around this house for weeks. Are you guys not hanging out together anymore?"

Greg said, "Oh Mom, Jeff is such a dweeb. He always has his face stuck in a book. He's no fun, and some of the guys are saying he's queer. I don't need to be associated with a weirdo. It could ruin my reputation. Lay off, Mom, I have other better friends that definitely know how to party and have fun."

Susie stopped Greg, "Hey, this dweeb has been your best friend for years. And this isn't like you to dump a good friend or let others put him down and start rumors. Where is your sense of loyalty to an old friend who has always had your back?"

Greg just shrugged and said, "I've changed, Mom. Boy have I changed. I have new friends, cooler friends, and my life is just going in a different direction than Jeff's. See you later, Mom." And he headed upstairs. As soon as Susie closed the front door, Greg pulled out his vial of pills to see how many he had left. He was going to need some cash to up his supply. This habit was a little pricier than he had thought in the beginning, or maybe he was taking more. Or maybe his supplier was giving him a weaker strength.

Yeah, that must be it; he was taking the same amount. One in the morning to get him going, one or two at lunch to get him through the afternoon, and then two before dinner, so he could stand to be around his parents and do his homework in the evening. He had found out from his new friends that if you mixed the pills with a beer or vodka, the affect was even better. He liked to fly high, and his old friend Jeff never even got off the ground. Hey, he thought, that was pretty funny.

Greg remembered that his mom had some really cool jewelry that her mother had left her, a diamond broach and a couple of rings. She never wore the broach or the rings, she'd never miss them, and he figured they were insured. He didn't need to sell them now, but it was good to know they were there if he needed more cash.

Susie apologized to Jay for being fifteen minutes late as she sat down at their favorite table way in the back of the darkest area of the wine bar. She told Jay that her son had been late coming home, and she wanted to touch base with him. She admitted to Jay that she was concerned about Greg's behavior.

"He seems to have changed so much in the last month or so. He's kind of a smart-ass, jittery, and is gone more than he's home. He has dumped his old friends and won't bring his new friends around. Is this normal behavior for a fifteen-year-old boy? Hormones? Or just a teenage boy being a teenage boy? What do you think, Jay, should I be worried?"

Jay thought about it for a minute and told Susie, "I would keep an eye on him. Boys that age are easily tempted or persuaded by their peers, and he could get into something way over his head. Boys that age think they know it all and are vulnerable to outside influences. Do you think he might be drinking or maybe taking drugs?"

Susie gave Jay a shocked look and said, "No way, Greg would never do drugs. He's way too smart for that. I do worry, though, that he doesn't bring home his new friends. I will suggest he invite them over so that I can meet them and I'll just be firmer with his hours. He's my only child, and I want the best for him. You're right, I need to keep vigilant, and I will sit him down tomorrow for a good talk. Now, tell me about your weekend."

Jay reached for Susie's hand and told her that his weekend had been lonely without her. He told her that he honesty was getting stronger feelings for her, and their friendship had deepened into something more serious. He didn't want to push her, but he wondered if maybe she felt the same way. He was willing to continue on the same, but he would like to take their relationship to the next level. He said, "I know you're married, but unhappily, and I'm not trying to break up your marriage. But I want to spend as much time with you as you'll allow. I have never met a woman as loving, warm, and sexy as you, and I think I'm falling in love with you."

Susie looked shocked and reached over to hold Jay's hand. "I care a great deal for you, more than I should, but I'm sixteen years older than you. You should be dating some nice woman your own age. I'm flattered, and I think you're wonderful. And yes, sometimes I want to take our relationship to the next level, but I'm not sure I'm ready to cheat on my husband or to become and adulteress. What do we do? What do you think we should do?"

Jay reached over and gave Susie a kiss on the cheek and told her, "Let's just play it by ear, one day at a time. We'll see each other like we are now, and if something more happens, well, so be it. And if nothing happens, we'll treasure our friendship. How does that sound to you?"

Susie agreed. She wasn't ready to give Jay up, and they agreed to meet again next week. And maybe once in a while, they can sneak in a second evening. This night, when Jay walked Susie to her car, he took her in his arms and kissed her deeply and whispered in her ear, "Take care of my girl, I need her."

As Susie drove home, she had a lot to think of. She was very glad that Mark wouldn't be home tonight; she needed time to herself. She knew she could be falling into a deep hole with no way out, and she wasn't sure she was ready to see that deep, dark hole. But the kiss left Susie feeling something that she hadn't felt for years. Desire—and it felt wonderful. She felt lighter and younger, and yes, sexier. Susie went right to bed without checking on Greg; after all, she had a lot on her mind. She just hollered a good night through Greg's door.

Joan

Joan fixed an early dinner on Thursday night since she had a bocce game that night. She left the roast on low on the stove, and she told Sandy that she could eat anytime, and Bob could reheat it when he got home from the hardware store. Bob seemed to be working later and later hours. The store was either very busy, or Bob preferred the nuts and bolts to home and hearth.

Joan wanted to get to bocce early since she had been late for practice on Tuesday night, and she had actually only spent twenty minutes practicing. She had gone furniture shopping in Napa with Frank after work. He needed a couch, a new mattress, and a few odds and ends to go with the furniture that he had shipped from his previous home. Frank wanted a new look that did not remind him of his deceased wife.

Joan had enjoyed the shopping and always had fun when she was with the doctor. He made her laugh and was always complimentary. He made her feel pretty and wanted. Bob never complimented her anymore, unless it was her meatloaf or lasagna. He said she was a better cook than his mother.

Now, that was what every woman wants to hear: "Your gravy makes my heart beat faster" or "Your spaghetti sauce makes me cry with joy." *Really, really, give me a break,* she thought. *I work my ass off at work every day, taking care of sick people, then I come home to "What's for dinner?"* How nice would it be if Bob would take her out to dinner once in a while? When she suggested that they go out for dinner, he would ask why, since she cooked better than most chefs and their kitchen was cozier. So in the end they stayed home, and she cooked, and cooked, and then cooked some more. And then on other days she baked, wow, what a varied life she lived; if you could call this living.

Despite the lack of practice, the women won all three games and were in great spirits when they headed for their usual spot for wine. Once they each ordered their favorite wine, they started filling each other in on what had happened in their lives in the last week since they had last talked. Normally they spoke on the phone every few days, but this week, they had each been busy with their own lives and just hadn't reached out to each other.

Joan led off with "Okay, ladies, how was your week? And what is new in your exciting lives? I will start off, and then each of you feel free to jump in."

Joan then told them about Dr. Frank Harris and how nice he was and how she had helped him find a house and new furniture. The other ladies were shocked. "Wow," Susie said, "sly you, spending time with a man other than Bob. I am so impressed."

Joan blushed and told them that she was just being a good friend. Frank was new to the hospital and town, and it was just the right thing to do, lend a helping hand.

Susie jumped in, "Make sure it's just your hand you loan him. So what does he look like? How old is he? Is he single, have kids? Come on, give us the dirt."

Joan playfully slapped at Susie's hand and said, "Don't make it sound like more than it is." She then filled the others in, that Frank was a widower, tall, rather nice looking, and gave his approximate age, since she had not asked to see his driver's license or birth certificate. But yes, she thought he was a few years older than she.

Barb told the others, "Well, I think it's nice that Joan has a new male friend. I would like to have a man that I could talk to once in a while. I would like to have an intelligent conversation with another adult, discuss other topics than wine grapes, and will the weather destroy this year's crops?" The girls were fun but not exactly well informed on politics or world affairs. "Once in a while, I would like to have a stimulating conversation."

Barb said, "Speaking of other men, Susie, are you still spending time with that young man? What's his name? Jay? If I remember right, you were mentoring him in all the ways to make wine? Or are you two making something other than wine now?"

Susie laughed, and said, "Yes, I'm still seeing Jay once in a while, but it's pretty much just professional chitchat. We share a lot of the same interests, and at least he listens to me. And he finds me attractive. Those are words I never hear anymore, especially from my husband. It's all harmless, but yes, it feels good to be admired. I don't see any harm in seeing him once in a while."

Maggie jumped in, "Well, make sure that Jay knows it's harmless, and don't give him the wrong idea. After all, he is young and impressionable. Lead with your head and not your heart is my motto. Actually, I'm a wee bit jealous of Susie and Joan. Both have new men in their lives. I have a husband that doesn't know if I'm alive and would probably prefer if I wasn't. Hey, Joan, does Frank have a single male friend? Or maybe Jay has a young stud for me."

The other three women just laughed and decided to call it a night. It was almost nine thirty, and each of them had to work the next day, and Joan got up especially early. They gave each other a hug as they walked to their cars. Joan yelled out, "See you Tuesday night for bocce practice." As Joan drove home, she wondered if Bob was home from the store yet, and if she would find a stack of dirty dishes to deal with as usual.

CHAPTER 18

Barb

When Barb got home on Thursday night after a pleasant evening with her three friends, she felt lighter and more hopeful. Maybe things would get better; she would talk to Jack over the weekend and make him understand how his drinking was hurting the family. He would have to listen. After all, the girls were the most important people in both of their lives. She also felt a little envious of Joan and Susie, with their friendships with men that were not their husbands. Barb would love to have a man to talk to that she didn't have to watch every word she spoke, so that she wouldn't set off his anger.

Barb checked on the girls, and as normal Lacey had locked her bedroom door but did respond with a good night, when her mother knocked on her door and told her good night and lights out. Brenda and Rachel shared a bedroom, and Rachel was reading a Nancy Drew book, and Brenda was texting a friend. Barb sat down on the side of Rachel's bed and told her that she had grown up reading Nancy Drew. Her own mother had passed most of the original hardcover books down to her. She had loved the stories of Nancy and her friends, Beth and George, solving the mysteries that they always found themselves embroiled in. Rachel asked her mom, "Why did they call Nancy's car a roadster and not a car? And why did they wear frocks and not dresses or pants?" Barb just laughed and explained that the Nancy Drew books had originally been written in the 1930s and that was the way they spoke in those days. But she had found the different language charming and fun.

Barb asked the girls if they had spent any time with Lacey, but they told her that Lacey had gone upstairs right after dinner and closed and locked her door. Brenda told Barb that she thought Lacey was being a brat, and she wouldn't help with the dishes. Lacey also said, "Dad called, and he said he was working late and not to wait up." Barb tucked the girls in bed and kissed them good night.

Barb was lying awake when Jack came to bed at twelve thirty. Barb pretended to be asleep rather than deal with Jack and get into a fight. She could tell he'd been drinking a lot from the way he was stumbling around the room and mumbling under his breath. Once he was in bed, he fell asleep immediately, snoring loudly. Barb just turned on her side and cried. She wondered, *Would things ever change? How can I deal with Jack and Lacey?* She knew something was going on with Lacey, but if Lacey wouldn't talk with her, what could she do?

The next morning, Barb got up early to make sure the girls had a good breakfast, and she wanted to have a chance to talk to Lacey before Lacey left for school. When Lacey came down, she was wearing a loose sweatshirt over baggy jeans, and her hair looked like it hadn't been brushed in days. Barb pulled Lacey into her arms and said, "Honey, what's going on? You have changed drastically in the last few weeks. Is something going on with school? Are you having problems with a boy? Are you being bullied by another girl? As a teacher, I see all kinds of bad behavior by kids, and we can deal with whatever is bothering you if you will just share the problem with me and your dad."

Lacey just pulled away and told her that there was nothing that her mother could do. She said, "If I have a problem, which I don't, I can handle it by myself." She then turned and walked out the door without even looking at her breakfast. Barb knew something was definitely going on with Lacey and made a promise to herself that she would go over to the high school after school ended and talk to Lacey's counselor. Maybe Mrs. Elliott would have some idea of what was going on with Lacey.

Barb dropped Brenda off at her school, and then she and Rachel drove to the elementary school. She walked Rachel to her class and then continued on to her own classroom. She was resolute that she would see Lacey's counselor right after she dropped off Rachel at home. She phoned Mrs. Elliott and made an appointment to see her at four in the afternoon in her office.

When Barb met with Mrs. Elliott and explained the sudden change in Lacey's behavior, she asked Mrs. Elliott if she had noticed any change in Lacey or had heard any rumors about bullying or problems with Lacey and another student. Mrs. Elliott told Barb that she had noticed a change in Lacey's attitude and her appearance. She had not heard about any problems with Lacey or her friends, but she would make some quiet inquiries and see if there were any rumors going around about Lacey. She told Barb that she usually heard the rumors of bullying, or who broke up with whom, etc. The school was like a small village, and everybody knew everyone else's business. She thought it wouldn't take her too long to find out what was going on with Lacey. She also suggested calling Lacey into her office and just asking her what was going on. But Barb didn't think that was a good idea yet. Barb would try to talk to Lacey again herself. Barb thanked Mrs. Elliott and told her that she'd keep in touch, and Barb headed home.

When Jack came home from work at six, Barb pulled him aside and shared her concerns about Lacey. Lacey had come home from school around five and had gone right to her room. She had told Barb that she had been at the library, and she had a big report do and would be in her room studying. Barb explained to Jack how worried she was and told him, "Something is really bothering Lacey. She's always been so easygoing, and now she is just shutting down and shutting us out. We have to do something before we lose her."

Lacey went upstairs, locked her bedroom door, and pulled out the stash of razor blades that she had stolen from her father's bathroom. Lacey pulled down her jeans and made a slash across her thigh. The cut made her eyes water, and there was some bleeding, but overall, it felt good. This was a pain she could control, unlike the pain that she endured in Mr. Martin's biology class. He had kept Lacey after class again that afternoon and had pulled up Lacey's sweatshirt and pulled down her jeans. He also opened his pants and shoved Lacey's hand in until she was touching his private area. Lacey tried to recoil and pull her hand back, but Mr. Martin's hand became even firmer, and he told Lacey that it was time she knew what a real man felt like, and she'd better get used to it, because soon he would have even bigger and better surprises for her. He again reminded her to keep her mouth shut, or he would destroy her family. When he was satisfied, he told Lacey she could leave, but told her to remember that no one would ever believe her story, so she'd better keep her pretty mouth shut. In the beginning she had started the cutting and baggy clothes as a deterrent to Mr. Martin, but that hadn't worked. Mr. Martin really didn't care if Lacey was crazy or not, as long as she was willing. Now the cutting had become a habit, a release of the fear that she felt all day. She had control over her body, and she could decide when and if she felt pain. She would stop this once the school year was over and she was no longer in Mr. Martin's class and no longer under this thumb. She wondered how many other girls had suffered his disgusting fondling over the years.

"Oh my god, Barb," Jack said, "you are just such a worrier. You invent things to worry about so you can solve them and be the hero. She's fine, just growing up and going through the normal growing pains. You need to just leave her alone and get off her back. And while you're at it, you can get off my back too."

Jack pulled a beer out of the refrigerator and went into the living room and told Barb to call him when dinner was ready. He wanted to read the paper and watch the news. He smirked at Barb. "I'm sure the TV news is a hell of a lot more exciting than the news around this house."

Barb thought to herself, *Well, I'm not giving up on Lacey even if her father has. I'm a teacher, and I know when a student is in trouble. And Lacey is in trouble. I will get to the bottom of this come hell or high water.* She would give Joan a call in the morning and ask Sandy to have another chat with Lacey. She set the table and then finished putting dinner on the table.

CHAPTER 19

Maggie

Saturday night, Maggie and Tom went out to dinner. She brought up the subject of Jeff and how she had been worried about him and that she had asked Michael to have a talk with Jeff. She told Tom that Jeff had seemed in a better mood once he had spent some time with Michael. She had asked Michael what was bothering Jeff, but he had just shrugged it off to teenage years. Michael had assured Maggie that Jeff was going to be fine and that Jeff would reach out to his parents when and if he had something to say.

Tom agreed with Michael that Jeff would be fine and was just going through puberty and the normal growing pains. Tom remembered his own youth and how difficult school had been and him trying to keep up his grades, so he could get into dental school and also play on the football team. "Of course," he said, "I was also trying to date on the weekends and keep up my image of the hottest guy on campus. I tell you, those were tough years."

Maggie hoped Tom was right, and Jeff was just feeling the pressure of school and trying to keep up his grades. She did share with Tom that she was concerned that he had not been dating. "Do you think that maybe he doesn't like girls, or could be possibly be gay?"

"I don't know. But I would think a boy his age would be on the phone constantly with girls and be asking for the car to take girls out."

"Speaking of, we talked about taking Jeff to look at buying him a used car now that he's sixteen and got his license. What about next weekend?" She asked. "Will that work for you?"

Tom gave Maggie a look of horror and told her, "My son is not gay. No son of mine would dare be gay. I will not tolerate it. I can assure you that he's a normal guy, with normal desires. He's probably just studying hard to get into a good college. You don't know what happens in school. He probably has the girls falling all over him. But I agree, let's take him car shopping next weekend. Cars are a chick magnet, and I remember the good times I had in the back seat of my first car. That reminds me. I'll pick up a box of condoms for Jeff, he needs to be prepared. I don't want him getting trapped by some girl and ruining his future."

Maggie agreed that, yes, Jeff needed to be protected, and the condoms would be a better idea coming from his dad than his mom. She then went on to ask Tom about the office and his patients. She asked him if he had found a new dentist to come into the practice. She knew that his practice had grown, and he was getting overwhelmed. The founding partner had retired the year before. His nurse Becky and his hygienist Sandy were helpful, but he really needed another dentist to give him a break and possibly a day off or a vacation.

Tom told her that he would be interviewing some new dentists the following week, and one woman in particular, Dr. Sharon Nelson, had come highly recommended to him and was willing to move from Reno to St. Helena to join a smaller practice. Tom was hopeful that she would work out, and he could actually take a day off once in a while during the week. Tom always hoped that Michael would make it through dental school and come into the practice with his dad. Who knows, maybe someday Jeff would come into the practice too.

Tom was very pleasantly surprised when he met and interviewed Dr. Sharon Nelson. He found her to be a smart and very pretty woman in her late thirties. Dr. Nelson was single and told him that she was anxious to move out of Reno and start life in a new town. She had just gotten out of a long-term relationship, and she was ready to move on to greener pastures. After reviewing her qualifications again, and her performance in the oral interview, Tom asked Dr. Nelson if she would like to join his practice.

Sharon, Dr. Nelson, quickly responded that she would be delighted and could move to St. Helena within the next few weeks. She would look for a small house to rent, and in the meantime, she could stay at a local B&B. She was excited to live and work in the charming little town, and she had heard wonderful stories of the wine and food.

Sharon filled out the necessary paperwork before leaving the office and promised to be at the office in two weeks. She told Tom she traveled light, with few possessions and one sweet cat. She shook Tom's hand and told him that she had a good feeling about him and thought they were going to be really good friends. Tom readily agreed; she would definitely make coming to work more fun, and she was certainly nice to look at.

Tom told Maggie that night that the new dentist, Dr. Nelson, had been hired and he had high hopes for her contribution to the practice. Maggie asked Tom what Dr. Nelson looked like and how old she was. Tom told Maggie that she was just average, sort of attractive, but he didn't find her pretty. Tom thought to himself, no sense in telling Maggie how pretty that Sharon really was. He wasn't really attracted to her, was he? It would just be nice to have a younger, more vibrant person in the office. That's all.

Maggie brought up the subject of Jeff again to Tom, and she asked him if he had talked to Jeff about, you know, girls, dating, condoms, etc. Maggie told Tom, "It would be easier for you to talk to him about this than me. Now that you're getting some help in the office, maybe you can spend more time with Jeff and possibly take him to a Giants game or go bowling. You know, do some father-and-son stuff"

Tom promised Maggie that he would try to spend more time with Jeff once Sharon became familiar with the office, and he would take Jeff car shopping the following weekend. Jeff hadn't been pushing yet for his own car, but both Maggie and Tom thought having his own car would give Jeff the incentive to maybe start dating and give Jeff the validation that his parents trusted him.

"Thanks, Tom, I think a car would really boost Jeff's mood. And we gave Michael a car when he turned sixteen. Gosh, Tom." Maggie laughed. "Do you remember the clunker Michael ended up getting? A Chevy Malibu, dented and ugly as sin, but she ran like a dream. Well, most of the time, and she got him where he needed to go. Do they still make Malibus? Maybe take him to a car lot in Napa, where there's bound to be a bigger inventory. I can't wait for you to tell Jeff. He'll be so excited."

Susie

Susie and Jay continued to meet on Monday nights at their little wine bar. The owner of the bar was fairly new to town, so Susie was not worried about being recognized. And if she was, she thought, who would care? If was just a harmless meeting with a fellow professional and winemaker. Even Susie didn't believe it was harmless anymore, but she loved spending time with Jay, and she wasn't ready to give him up. He was the opposite of Mark; Jay was kind, considerate, and treated her like a woman. Mark treated her like a possession, not even a wife, but just something he owned. Mark wasn't even particularly nice to his own son anymore; he ignored Greg as much as he did her. *What is going on with Mark, anyway?* she thought. *I doubt that he's that busy at work.* I wonder if he has a little somebody on the side. Which, if true, made Susie feel more entitled to see Jay. What's good for the goose is good for her, she rationalized.

Jay told Susie how much he had missed her that week and could they maybe find another night to spend together, maybe spend a Sunday out of town in San Francisco, or maybe drive up the coast to Mendocino? "Susie," Jay said, "just think about it. We could have a picnic and spend the whole day really getting better acquainted. What do you think? Can you get away maybe on a Saturday or Sunday?"

Susie thought about it for a minute, and she loved the idea of spending a whole day with Jay. "Okay," she said, "but not San Francisco, that's Mark's turf. But Mendocino sounds good. Mark plays golf on some Saturday mornings, and once in a while on

Sunday. I'll find out when he's playing again and let you know. I can tell Mark and Greg that I'm meeting an old school friend in Santa Rosa for a day of shopping. Honestly, Mark doesn't care what I do anyway. So yes, I would love to. I'll text you when I know what day works best."

With that settled, they spent the rest of their evening chatting and holding hands under the table. Susie looked at Jay and suggested that maybe he should spend more time with other women, other younger women. Her suggestion was half-hearted, but she wanted to be fair and give him the option to date other women if he chose. After all, she was not free, and maybe Jay would like to get married someday and have children. Even if she wasn't married, she was too old to have babies.

Jay gave her hand a squeeze and told her that he had never pictured himself as a Dad, and younger women weren't as exciting or as smart as Susie. He told her that he had always been attracted to older women. "You're stuck with me, Susie, at least as long as you still want me," Jay explained.

Susie and Jay stayed at the wine bar later than usual, and when they got to the dark parking lot, Jay gave Susie another long, tender kiss. Susie kissed Jay back and whispered to him, "I swear, Jay, your kisses are curling up my toenails. I don't think my heart can take this much excitement. I can't wait to spend a whole day with you, and I will text you as soon as I can find a full day that I can get away." With one final kiss, they each drove away.

When Susie got home, she was surprised to see Mark home reading the local newspaper. Mark casually asked Susie where she had been. "Oh," she lied, "I had an extra bocce practice. We're playing a really tough team this Thursday, and we thought we should get in another day of practice. Where is Greg, is he already in bed?"

Mark gave Susie a dismissive look and told her that Greg had just gotten home and had gone straight upstairs to bed. Greg had told Mark that he had a lot of homework. Mark was curious if Susie was spending too much time at bocce and with her friends and not keeping a close eye on Greg. He thought Greg had been acting kind of odd lately, and maybe Susie needed to see if Greg was having trouble in school. He asked Susie if she had checked on Greg's grades lately. And was he still as involved in after-school sports?

Susie told Mark, "Well, if you're so concerned, you could spend some time with your son. You could go to games with him and offer to help with his homework. In other words, Mark, you could give a damn too and be a responsible dad. He's your son too. You are gone more than you're home. If you're not working, you're golfing. As a family, we don't exist anymore."

Mark just frowned at Susie and told her to stop being so dramatic. "Speaking of being gone, I have a business meeting in Chicago this weekend, so I'm leaving Friday morning and won't be home until late Sunday night. So don't count on me this weekend. Someone has to support this family. You may keep us stocked with wine, but I'm the one who brings in the bacon."

Mark's words stung. He always seemed to find a way to belittle her, to put her in her place. Susie had worked hard to be a great winemaker, college, internship, and then fighting her way up the ladder in a man's world, rung by rung. Why didn't Mark see that? Why couldn't he appreciate her? Susie just ignored Mark's biting words and went upstairs to check on Greg and say good night.

Susie knocked on Greg's door and said good night. "Honey, do you need anything before I go to bed? Did you have dinner? Can I make you a sandwich?"

"No!" Greg yelled, "I'm good. Just talking to one of the guys while I do my homework." Actually, Greg was trying to hold his shaking hands steady, and he could feel his heart racing. *It must have been the last two pills I took*, he thought. *I should have just taken one.* His friend that had sold him the pills had warned him only to take one at a time. But Greg had been down about the D on his history test and needed a pickup, so he had taken two pills. He needed something to calm him down; he had heard about kids having heart attacks. He remembered that his mom had a prescription for Ativan in her bathroom that had been ordered when she had a minor surgical procedure. Maybe one or two of those would calm him down. It was worth a try, and he went into his mother's bathroom when she went downstairs to get a book to read. Sure enough, within fifteen minutes, he could feel his heart returning to normal. Okay, now he knew not to take more than one pill at a time. The high was great, but the side effects weren't cool at all. He would have to be more careful in the future.

As Susie climbed into bed, she thought, *Well, I guess I can spend a day this weekend with Jay in Mendocino, since Mark is going to be gone all weekend.* She thought she would spend one day with Jay and one day with Greg. She had been putting Greg on the back burner lately, which was unusual for Susie; normally, she was a great Mom and loved spending time with Greg. Maybe they could spend the whole day together and then go out for a really nice dinner. She would make it up to him, she promised herself. Susie fell asleep long before Mark came to bed.

Mark was downstairs sitting in his chair, watching the late news, and thinking about the great weekend he had planned with his secretary, Kim. He really didn't need to take Kim to the meeting; in fact, the meeting really wasn't essential. He could have handled the client by e-mail or a conference call, but he thought it would be a good excuse to get away and find out how much Kim really liked him. He had booked two rooms at the hotel but hoped only one would be needed. When he had asked Kim to accompany him, she seemed to understand that this was more than business. But then again, you never know; women can be so unpredictable.

CHAPTER 21

Joan

Joan's workweek had been busy, and she was looking forward to a weekend off, and maybe she and Sandy could drive to Napa and take Brad out to lunch on either Saturday or Sunday. Maybe Bob would like to join them, and they could have a real family day. She would check with both of them and see if they had plans. Sandy often spent the weekends with dates or friends, and Bob often worked, but maybe he could leave the store for a few hours with the employees.

When she got home on Friday night and started dinner, she texted Sandy to see if she was free on either day to have lunch or dinner with Brad, depending on his work schedule. They hadn't seen Brad since he had come by to show them his new motorcycle. She missed spending time with her oldest son, her firstborn; they had always been so close.

Sandy texted back that she was sorry, but she had made plans for both days but maybe next weekend. She was out for dinner with friends. When Bob walked in, he grabbed a beer out of the fridge and asked when dinner would be ready. There was a game on TV that he wanted to catch the end of. Joan then suggested to Bob that they drive to Napa on either Saturday or Sunday and spend some time with their son. "Oh gosh," Bob said, "I'm having a big paint sale this weekend, and I need to be at the store both days, maybe next weekend."

Great, Joan thought, *well, I will just give Brad a call and go by myself.* She texted Brad and asked if he was free either day for lunch, and she was elated when Brad texted back that Saturday at noon would work but that he had to be a work by three. "Perfect," she told him, "I'll meet you at the restaurant at noon." She then told him about the new restaurant on the Napa River that she had heard such good things about. They served French food and were open for lunch and dinner.

On Saturday, Joan got to the restaurant a few minutes before Brad and secured a table by the window overlooking the river. Brad arrived a few minutes later and gave his mom a big hug as he sat down. Joan told Brad how good he looked even if his hair was a little longer than the last time she had seen him. She was curious if the long hair bothered his bosses at the bar. "Hell no," Brad told his mom, "they think it attracts the younger set, and as long as I keep it tied back, there is no problem."

Brad filled Joan in on his work and social life once they had placed their lunch orders. He asked Joan how life was at the hospital and how Sandy and his dad were doing. She told him that Sandy was busy with school and her dating life, and she didn't see as much of Sandy as she would like. Joan continued, "I barely see your dad at all. He lives at the store. He barely comes home to eat and sleep. I'm a hardware widow, but I guess I can't complain since the store is doing well. Oh, we do have a new doctor at the hospital, and he's very nice. I've been helping him settle in, so my life has a little bit of excitement in it."

Brad laughed and teased Joan about not getting too involved with the new doctor. Joan replied, "That's what your dad told me. He's sure Frank—Dr. Harris—will start bringing me his laundry."

"Wow, Mom, it's Frank now, not Dr. Harris. How friendly are you two? Should I be worried about Frank replacing Dad?"

Joan gave Brad a shove. "Really, Brad, Frank and I are just friends. He's new to St. Helena, and he needs a friend. He will make more friends once he's been here for a while."

Their lunch arrived, and the conversation turned to the food and how good it was. Brad thought that he should bring his girlfriend to the restaurant on his next night off. All too soon, it was two and time for Brad to leave for work. Brad gave Joan a big hug and told her that he'd come home for breakfast in the next couple of weeks. Joan told Brad, "Make sure you do, we all miss you."

Joan decided to do some window-shopping since she was already downtown, and she wanted to check out the little art gallery on First Street. She and Bob had been meaning to go for months but just hadn't found the time. Joan walked slowly over to First Street, enjoying the nice day, and looking in the shop windows.

Joan walked into the art store just as a man was walking out, almost knocking her flat. "Oh," the man said, "I am so sorry, I wasn't paying attention. Oh Joan, it's you."

Joan laughed. "Yes, Frank, it's me that you were trying to flatten. What are you doing in Napa? Aren't you on duty today?"

Frank told Joan that he was off today, and he thought he would look for some art for the living room. "I saw a few pieces I like in the store, but I want to think about it before I splurge." Frank asked Joan that if she had time to look at the artwork he was contemplating, he would appreciate a woman's opinion. Joan told Frank that she would love to; she was going to browse in the little shop anyway.

Frank led Joan back into the store and over to one of the paintings that he liked. It was a landscape of the valley and the vineyards on an early foggy morning. It was absolutely beautiful. Frank looked at Joan, "Well, Ms. Art Expert, what do you think? I was thinking about putting it over the couch. And then there is a smaller one of a hot-air balloon over the valley that I would like to hang in the hall. Please give me your honest opinion. You won't hurt my feelings. Maybe the paintings but not mine."

Joan thought they were both perfect. She especially loved the larger landscape, and she told Frank that he had great taste. She knew that the colors in the picture would go well with his new couch, and he could pick up a few toss pillows to pull the colors all together. She told Frank that she thought he should go for it and buy them both.

"Okay, I will. Even though I may be broke for the next three months, eating only at the hospital cafeteria. I may force you to join me since it's your fault that I'm spending all this money." Frank gave the gallery owner his credit card, and they waited while she wrapped up the paintings. Once the paintings were secure, Joan helped Frank carry them to his car.

When the paintings were safely stowed away in the back seat, Frank asked Joan if he could buy her a glass of wine in one of the numerous wine bars on First Street. After all, he told her, "You owe me, after you made me spend all that money. Or maybe I owe you for helping me out again. Either way, let's enjoy a glass of wine to celebrate my new artwork."

Joan told Frank okay, that she would be delighted, but he really didn't owe her or she didn't owe him, or nobody owed anyone. Joan led them down the street to a little wine bar on the corner. Joan had been at this wine bar before with Brad, and she knew they represented some nice wineries. They both ordered a glass of Chardonnay and settled down at one of the little bistro tables.

Frank asked Joan why she had been in Napa, and she told him that she had been having lunch with her son, Brad. She told him about the little French restaurant on the Napa River that she and Brad had eaten at. She suggested that Frank try it sometime. In fact, Napa has some wonderful restaurants, all within walking distance of each other. Frank said he would love to, but he hated to eat alone, so he might wait until he had made some friends. Unless Joan was willing to join him, and then he would love to try the French restaurant as well as some of the others she had suggested.

Joan just laughed and told Frank she'd think about it. They spent the next hour just chatting about wine, restaurants, and books and movies that they both enjoyed. She told Frank that she loved old movies and musicals and enjoyed going to San Francisco to catch the occasional play. Frank told her he also enjoyed Broadway musicals and plays and also liked old movies, but his preference ran to James Cagney, Humphrey Bogart, and Jimmy Stewart. He told her he could also get into a good mystery and the occasional western. He told Joan he was a man of varied tastes.

After a great afternoon, Frank walked Joan back to her car and thanked her again for a great afternoon. He gave her a quick hug and said, "We'll have to do this again. I had a wonderful time." Joan agreed that it had been the perfect afternoon, and she would see him at the hospital on Monday. She was thoughtful on the way back up to St. Helena, asking herself why Bob couldn't be more spontaneous and like to do the things that she liked to do. All Bob wanted to do was work. When was the last time they had gone to the city for a play or even the last time they had gone out to a nice restaurant for dinner? Didn't he care about her anymore?

Barb

Barb gave Joan a call on Monday evening and asked Joan to have Sandy call Lacey at her convenience. She told Joan what was going on with Lacey and how worried she was. Barb told Joan, "I know something serious is going on with Lacey, more than schoolwork or boys, and I need Sandy's help in finding out what it is. Lacey has always looked up to Sandy, and I know that she'll listen to Sandy and hopefully tell her what's going on with her and why she has changed so drastically."

Joan promised she would speak to Sandy as soon as she got home and ask her to reach out to Lacey. Barb thanked Joan and asked her how her weekend had been. Joan told Barb briefly about having lunch with Brad and then running into Frank and helping him shop for artwork.

Barb told Joan that her weekend had been more fun than hers had been. "Lacey spent the weekend in her room, Jack was either working or out with his buddies, and I took Rachel and Brenda to the show and out for pizza." Oh, and then she had the pleasure of doing housework and laundry. She just felt so blessed. Barb didn't get into the fact that Jack spent much of his time drunk. She didn't want to hurt his reputation, but more than that, she didn't want to be embarrassed and have her friends know that her husband was a drunk and, worse, that she put up with it.

Jack was normally careful when he was around her friends or out in social situations, but once in a while he slipped and overimbibed when they were out, and then she had to make excuses for him. She was getting tired of covering his ass.

But right now, her first priority was Lacey. She had to find out what was going on in Lacey's life that had thrown her for such a loop. She had withdrawn from her entire family and friends, she wasn't eating, and she looked like hell. *God help me,* Barb thought, *what if Lacey's involved in drugs?*

When Brenda and Rachel were doing their homework, Barb tried to talk to Lacey in her room. Barb knocked on Lacey's door and asked Lacey if she could please come in. Lacey got up and opened the door and gestured for her mother to sit down on her bed and said, "What you do want, Mom? I have lots of homework to do."

Barb said, "Look, honey, I know something is going on in your life. Something is seriously bothering you, and I need to know what it is. I want to help you. Is it a boy? Is some kid bullying you? Please tell me you're not doing drugs. I can't believe I even asked that, but I have to. If you are involved in drugs, I can help you. No blame, just help, but please, please talk to me. Let me help you."

Lacey just looked at her mom with tears in her eyes. "Mom, I'm not doing drugs, and it's not a boy. And no, another student is not bullying me. I really don't want to talk about it. I can't really talk about it. Please just try to understand and just let me be. Hopefully everything will work out, but I just don't want to talk about it now. Please respect my privacy." Then Lacey gestured to the door for her mom to leave. Joan told her that she would leave her alone for now, but she expected Lacey to come to the table for dinner, and that she would be there to talk when Lacey was ready.

Lacey agreed to come down for dinner and then closed the door behind her mother. Once Joan left the room, Lacey sat down on the bed and cried. She would get through this school year. Once she was out of Mr. Martin's class, she would be free of him. Lacey then pulled the razor out from beneath her mattress and made a small cut in the back of her leg, where the scar wouldn't be seen. She thought to herself as she saw the blood bubble up: *See, Mr. Martin, I still have some control over my life and who has the final say in my pain.*

Barb went back downstairs to finish dinner and get it on the table. Jack wasn't home yet, but they were going to sit down to dinner with or without him. She called the girls to the table as she placed the roasted chicken and mashed potatoes down. If she did nothing else, she tried to feed her family healthy meals. She said a little prayer to herself as she waited for the girls to gather at the table.

Jack came in about ten with no apologizes. His breath smelled like liquor, but at least he wasn't staggering. He told Barb to heat him up a plate; he hadn't had time for dinner. Rather than argue with Jack, Barb went to the kitchen and reheated a plate of chicken and potatoes and set it down on the coffee table in front of the TV. She told him to enjoy, and she was going to bed.

Tuesday, Barb got a text from Sandy, saying that she would give Lacey a call and make a date to take Lacey to lunch the next weekend, that she was concerned about Lacey too. Barb texted back to Sandy: "Thank you, I don't know what else to do."

Barb made it to bocce practice on time after putting a hurried dinner on the table. Barb reminded Brenda to keep an eye on Rachel and on Lacey too. "Text me if you have a problem." Jack wasn't home from work yet. The other team members were already at the courts and ready to practice. Joan came over to Barb and gave her a hug and asked if there was any change with Lacey. "No," Joan told her, "no change." Barb told her she had tried to talk to Lacey over the weekend, but Lacey had basically blown her off.

Joan reassured Barb that Sandy would spend some time with Lacey next weekend, and God willing it would all work out. Joan gave Barb a quick squeeze and said "Hang on, kiddo, it will get better. I promise. Now put a fake smile on your face and get your ass on the court and practice."

Lacey did receive a call from Sandy to have lunch together the following Saturday. When Lacey tried to decline, Sandy told Lacey that she would come over and haul her butt out of the house even if she was in her pajamas, so finally Lacey agreed. She truly loved Sandy as a friend, and Lacey had always looked up to Sandy. To Lacey, Sandy had it all. She thought, Sandy wouldn't let Mr. Martin treat her like a slut and use her in his disgusting way. Maybe Lacey should tell Sandy what was going on, but no, if she did Mr. Martin would retaliate and get her mom fired. What a mess she was in. How had she ever got into this situation? Was Mr. Martin right that she was inviting his advances by the way she dressed, or the makeup that she wore? She didn't want to look like a slut; she just wanted to fit in with her friends. She had never had a boy treat her badly or call her names. What had she done to make Mr. Martin behave like this? Mr. Martin kept telling her it was her fault for flaunting herself, that she was trying to tempt the boys and him. Lacey kept thinking in her mind over and over: *It's my fault, my fault.* And she picked up the razor again.

Maggie

Tom and Maggie took Jeff car shopping in Napa on Saturday. They found a nice used Honda Civic with only forty-two thousand miles on it. The car had the minimum of dents, and the engine checked out well. Jeff said he liked it, and even the baby blue wasn't too bad. "Wow, such enthusiasm." Tom laughed.

Maggie said, "Honey, are you sure you like it? We can look at something else if you prefer a Jeep. Or maybe a small pickup?"

Jeff told Maggie that he really liked it, and could they take it with them today? Tom told him that that shouldn't be a problem once they signed the paperwork and offered proof of insurance and, yes, write them a check. Two hours later, Jeff drove his car off the lot, with Tom and Maggie following close behind. Maggie asked Tom, "Do you think Jeff's okay with the car and he's happy? He didn't seem exactly ecstatic. I just want him to be happy."

Tom just laughed at Maggie. "He's fine, Mags, he's just being cool. You know, not showing how excited he really is. He'll be home washing and waxing the car by tomorrow and then taking some of his buds out for a spin. Although I think I need to check the DMV book on how many passengers a young driver can have in his car. I think there's some kind of restriction on that."

When Maggie and Tom got home, Jeff was showing the car off to the neighbor girl. "See, Maggie, I told you so."

Maggie said, "You're right. I'll go get the car wax. By the way, Tom, I wanted to ask you how your new dentist Sharon is working out. Do you like her? Does your office staff like her? We need to invite her over for dinner once she gets settled."

Tom told Maggie that Sharon, Dr. Nelson, seemed to be working out. She saw a few patients this last week, and they seemed to like her. "I didn't hear any screaming, and no one ran out of the office. So overall I think she'll be good for the practice. I think we should hold off inviting her for dinner for a month or so, just until she gets settled."

Maggie told Tom, "You're the boss. Just let me know when you want to ask her over."

What Tom didn't tell Maggie was that he had taken Sharon for a two-hour lunch on Thursday. He told himself that he was just being welcoming, but he wondered if it was also because she was so pretty and, yes, alluring in her tight pants and white coat. He had to admit that he found Sharon entertaining and her conversation lively. He had thoroughly enjoyed their lunch and hoped to do it again soon. There was no harm in a simple little lunch with his employee, right?

Jeff asked Maggie and Tom if he could take his new car and go hang out with some friends, and he'd pick up a burger at the local A&W. He promised to be home by eleven, and both parents agreed.

Maggie asked Tom if he wanted to go out to dinner or maybe the movies in Napa, but Tom said he felt like staying home, and maybe just watch a movie on TV. He told her not to worry about a big dinner but maybe just soup and a grilled-cheese sandwich.

"Sure, Tom." Maggie was fine with an easy dinner. She pulled some soup out of the freezer and made grilled-cheese and tomato sandwiches, and they sat down with a bottle of wine for a quiet dinner. While Maggie was cleaning up the kitchen, Tom went into the den to watch the news on TV. When Maggie finished up in the kitchen, she joined Tom on the couch and reached over and nibbled on his ear and whispered, "Hey, cutie, do you want to go upstairs and fool around? We have the house alone for a few hours. What do you think?"

Tom gave Maggie a smile but told her he thought he would pass on her pass. "I had a hard week, and I'm feeling a little headachy."

Maggie looked disappointed but told Tom, "Hey, the headache is supposed to be my line, not yours. But I understand, I'll leave you alone. I've got a new book that I want to start anyway."

Tom felt guilty, but he just didn't feel romantic toward Maggie right now. He thought to himself, *It's just a temporary mood, Maggie is still very attractive.* But his mind kept slipping back to Sharon and how pretty she was, and she seemed to ooze raw sex appeal. He was pretty sure that Sharon was not aware of how sexy she was or how she came across.

Maggie curled up in a chair with her book, but her mind kept wandering to Tom and why he didn't seem interested in her anymore. She thought she still looked pretty good at forty-nine; she maintained her weight, kept her hair colored, and always wore makeup. *I may not be a babe anymore, but I'm not a dog either.*

Maybe I should show up at his office in a trench coat with nothing on underneath. Wow, that would go over big. I might make the local papers. I can see the headlines: "Dentist's wife does strip in office, patients run screaming from their chairs." Oh never mind, she thought, *I'll just wait up for Jeff. Maybe he'll sit down and talk with the old lady.*

Tom was in bed snoring when Jeff got home at eleven. Maggie asked Jeff if he'd had a good time, and what did his friends think of his new car? He told Maggie that he'd had fun, just went out with Sonny, one of his oldest friends. Maggie asked Jeff why he never spent time with Greg anymore. "You two used to be such good friends. Did you have a falling out?"

Jeff told his mom, "I hate to say this about Greg, but he's changed. He hangs with a bad crowd. Drinking, drugs, they cut class and are just losers. I worry that Greg is getting in over his head and maybe even doing drugs. I've invited him to hang out with me, but he just blows me off. So no, I'm not even trying anymore. Sorry, Mom, I know you are best friends with his mother, but I just don't like him anymore. And I sure don't want to hang with him and his gang buddies."

Maggie told Jeff that she was proud of him, and if he thought Greg was into something unsavory, then she was glad that Jeff had backed away from his old friend. Maggie also said that she would say something discreetly to Susie, without bringing Jeff into the conversation. Maggie didn't want anything bad to happen to Greg, and if he could be helped, she owed it to Susie to warn her. Maggie gave Jeff a big hug, told him to go to bed and not worry about it.

Jeff thought about what his mom had said about being proud of him. He wondered if she'd feel the same way if she knew that he might be gay. Would she think he was a queer? Would she be ashamed and stop loving him? His dad would be even worse; his dad always talked about what a stud he had been in high school and college, and how the girls were always chasing him. He even talked about his conquests in the back seat of his old car. Jeff didn't think he would be having any conquests in his new Honda. How did gay guys meet other gay guys? Do they go on Match.com or put an ad in the personal column? But then, Greg thought, maybe he really wasn't gay. Maybe he was a late bloomer, and he would start to like girls next week, or next year. A guy could only hope. This was his last thought as he fell asleep.

CHAPTER 24

Susie

After bocce on Thursday night, Susie joined her friends for their usual after-game glass of wine at their usual haunt. The girls had won all three games, so their spirits were high. As soon as they sat down and ordered their wine, Susie high-fived the ladies and said, "Woohoo! We did it! We cleaned their clock, wiped the floor with them, took them down. Those men looked totally pissed. I am so sorry—yeah right."

Barb told Susie, "I'm glad to hear that you're so humble. Your modesty doesn't become you." The other two women just laughed, but they agreed that it had been fun, beating the pants off the all-male team. Barb had to admit, though, that the men had put up a good fight, and all three games had been very close. But Barb said, "Back to reality. So what are everyone's plans for the weekend?"

Maggie told the others that her weekend would most likely be the same old, but if anyone wanted to go to the movies or go shopping, she was game. She thought, Tom would play golf and then probably tinker around the yard, so she would be available on Saturday morning. She suggested mani-pedis if anyone was interested.

Barb thought she would stay close to home; she was still worried about Lacey and wanted to keep a close eye on her. Joan knew that Lacey was having problems, but the others didn't, so Barb gave them a quick rundown on Lacey's behavior. Maggie jumped in with "You don't think she's doing drugs, do you? One of pharmacy representatives told me the other day that a rumor is going around about the kids at the high school doing street drugs. So hopefully Lacey's not involved in something like that."

Barb said, "No, I don't think it's drugs, but who can be sure? Joan's daughter, Sandy, has offered to talk to Lacey this weekend and see if she can find out what the problem is. Hopefully she'll have better luck than I have. God knows I've tried, but she just shuts me out. My heart is breaking, and I'm at such a loss."

Susie voiced her opinion. "Maybe it's just being a teenager, and Greg has been acting really weird lately too. He doesn't want to talk to Mark or me. He has totally checked out on us. I've been asking Mark to talk to him, but Mark is always too busy. In fact, he's going away this weekend on business, so I'm on my own. However, I'm thinking about making plans for Saturday or Sunday and hopefully one of the days Greg will spend with me. At least I'm going to try to persuade him to spend some time with the old lady."

Joan asked Susie, "Well, what about the other day? What are your plans?"

Susie just smiled and told her, "I'm still working on it. I may just drive up the coast a bit. You know, look at the ocean, relax, get in touch with my inner self."

"Speaking of inner self, Susie, are you still seeing Jay? Helping him with his work?" Joan asked.

Susie told them, "Yes, once in a while we get together for a glass of wine or coffee just to go over drip irrigation and other growing issues. No big deal."

Maggie said, "I wouldn't mind going over his growing issues, if you get my drift."

"Oh my gosh, Maggie, keep it clean please. My poor virgin ears," Joan said as she pretended to cover her ears.

The others just laughed and changed the subject to more mundane topics: work, cooking, politics, and life in general. They all agreed that life would be a lot less exciting without bocce and their friendship. They knew how lucky they were to have each other and their cherished friendship.

When Susie was driving home, all she could think about was the day she was going to spend with Jay on Saturday and their drive up the coast to Mendocino. Susie had asked Greg to spend Sunday with her, either going to the movies or maybe going to San Francisco for the day. He normally loved taking the ferry from Vallejo into the city. They could shop, have a good lunch, and maybe catch a ballgame or play. There were always lots to do in the city. Susie had been very disappointed when Greg told her that he had made plans to spend the day with his friends, but he promised his mom that they would have bonding time soon. Yeah right, Susie thought to herself.

Mark left early Friday morning for his trip, and Susie reminded him to call when he arrived safely and reminded him that he needed to spend time with Greg the next weekend. Tom promised he would spend time with Greg soon, gave her a quick kiss on the cheek, and was out the door. Susie still remembered the days when Mark could barely tear himself away from her. Now he could barely spend time with her. When had their lives changed? Had they stopped loving each other or just didn't like each other anymore? Did all couples go through this midlife boredom?

On Saturday morning, Susie parked her car in a grocery store parking lot in Calistoga, so no one would see her climb into Jay's car. They had agreed to meet at eight and then drive slowly up the coast and find a quiet spot to picnic with an ocean view.

She found Jay's car easily, and as she fastened her seatbelt, she looked at Jay and said, "Are you sure we should be doing this? I know it's harmless, but yet I feel kind of funny about it. I really don't think Mark would approve, and actually I don't think my friends would approve either. What do you think?"

Jay said, "Look, Susie, we're both adults. And we don't have to do anything we don't want to do. We enjoy each other's company, and I just don't see the harm in it. Let's just relax and enjoy the day, and we'll see what happens or doesn't happen. Just loosen up and enjoy the drive. I brought a nice picnic of chicken sandwiches, fruit, cookies, and a bottle or two of cold wine, and two blankets to spread out our gourmet lunch. It should take up two and a half to three hours to get there, so hang on and enjoy. The best is yet to come."

Susie agreed with Jay that they were both adults, and nothing would happen that they didn't want to happen. So she just lay her head back and turned on the radio to some soft music and let her mind clear of any worries.

Jay found a quiet hill overlooking the beach. There were no other people in site. The weather was pleasant and sunny, with just a hint of chill in the air. They spread out the blanket and set out the food that Jay had so neatly packed in a small ice chest. Jay had admitted that he had picked up the food from a little deli on Main Street. He told Susie he had many talents, but cooking wasn't one of them. He poured each of them a glass of wine, and then he invited her to stretch out and enjoy the view.

Susie had to admit, it was absolutely beautiful: the ocean and the wispy, windblown trees. It was almost eerie in the wild yet peaceful beauty. Susie had always loved the sharp lines of the rugged coastline. She just lay on the blanket watching the hawks and seagulls fly overhead.

The lunch was delicious, and they lingered over a second bottle of cold Sauvignon Blanc. Susie had to admit that this had been a wonderful idea. Jay leaned over Susie and gave her a slow, tender kiss, and when Susie leaned into Jay, the kisses became more ardent. And soon Jay was touching Susie and unbuttoning her blouse. Susie started to whisper no, but then Jay kissed her again, and all thoughts of right and wrong flew out of her head. She wanted Jay more than she could imagine. For the first time in years, she felt loved, desirable, and yes—young and beautiful again.

Jay pulled another blanket over them, and they made love on the grassy hillside with only the birds as witnesses. It was a moment neither of them would ever forget. They lay there in silence for a few minutes, just basking in their emotions. Finally, Susie sat up and pulled on her clothes. She looked at Jay and said, "I should say I'm sorry, but I'm not. I guess when I agreed to come with you, I knew this might happen. I didn't want to face it, but in the back of my mind I knew I wanted to be with you."

Jay pulled her close and told her that he was not sorry, and that he thought he was falling in love with her. He knew it was more than a fling, more than sex, even though it was the best sex he had ever had. He said, "I don't know how this will turn out, but I'm not going to give you up easily. At any time and for any reason you want me to back off, I will, but otherwise I will pursue you with all the love in my heart. Got that, Susie? I don't quit easy. Now we better get on the road before your son calls out the highway patrol."

Both were quiet on the drive back to Calistoga. Susie was thinking about what they had just done. She was, in essence, an adulteress, a married woman who had cheated on her husband. Was she a whore, a slut, or just a very unhappy woman in an unhappy marriage? She had a lot to think about. Did she stay with Mark to try to put their marriage back together? And could she give up Jay and the joy that he gave her?

Jay knew that Susie had a lot to think about, so he was content just to let her sit in silence. And he to deal with his own thoughts. He was not normally a home-wrecker; he had never gone after a married woman before. But he had never felt this way about a married woman before. Susie was different: she was warm, intelligent, and beautiful. He had felt something special the minute he met her. What would happen to them in the future was anyone's guess, but he was ready for the long fight if that was what it took.

When they arrived back in Calistoga, Jay gave Susie a kiss, and told her, "Please don't give up on us. Please don't ever feel guilty. What we did was out of love and mutual respect. Please let's just see what happens. I'll let you think about us on Sunday, and I will see you Monday night at the usual time and place. Be kind to yourself, you'll do the right thing."

When Susie got home, she called out to Greg. But apparently, he was out again. She found a note that Greg had left, telling her he was going bowling in Napa with some friends. He might be late, so not to worry.

In Chicago, Mark and Kim had just gotten back to their hotel after a nice dinner. Mark invited Kim up to his room for a brandy. Kim agreed, and soon they were settled with a glass of brandy, and Mark had turned on some soft music. Kim looked at Mark, smiled, and said, "If I didn't know better, I would think you were attempting to hit on me, but I'm sure I must be wrong."

Mark walked over, touched Kim's shoulder, and answered her, "If I was hitting on you, would I succeed or would I strike out? You're a beautiful young woman, and I do find you very desirable. In fact, so desirable that I was thinking of promoting you at the office. You are much more to me than an assistant or secretary. What do you think, are you ready for more responsibility?"

Kim walked over and put her arms around Mark and whispered in his ear, "More ready than you know." Mark led Kim into the bedroom, and the subject of the promotion had been decided.

Greg, walked into the house well after midnight, and it looked like he had lucked out—the house was dark, and his mom must have gone to bed. Greg was feeling edgy and his skin felt itchy like it had been burnt. It had been hours since he and the guys had taken the pills washed down with the tequila, but it was taking longer to come down this time than the last time. He had noticed that his face was starting to twitch around his mouth. Maybe he was just getting some bad stuff; he thought he would talk to the other guys tomorrow to see if they were feeling funny too.

Greg knew his parents would be upset if they knew he was doing drugs, but his new friends had said the drugs were harmless, and all the guys were doing it. Greg was starting to get worried, though. His grades the last month, were in the dumper, and he was cutting as many classes as he attended. He was also having a hard time sleeping and had dropped some weight. He would have to take another one of his mom's Ativan if he could get in and out of her bathroom without waking her. What the hell, he thought, if she does wake up, he could just say he was looking for aspirin.

When Greg tiptoed into his mother's room, she was breathing softly, and he was able to get in it, grab the bottle of the pills, and get back out without waking her. She had six pills left in the bottle, and he thought he had better keep it with him in case he needed it again. He would ask Frankie, the man that sold them the other drugs, if maybe he could buy some Ativan and keep it on hand just in case. He was also going to need more cash if he was going to maintain his stash. *Hey,* he thought, *that's funny, cash and stash. Damn, I'm funny.* Greg quickly swallowed the Ativan with a Coke, and hopefully the jitters would go away and he could sleep. As he was drifting off, he began to wonder if this road he had started on with his new friends might not be the best road to follow.

Sunday morning, Susie offered to either take Greg out to breakfast or fix whatever he wanted to eat: waffles, pancakes, or bacon and eggs. But Greg just shook his head. "Just juice and a piece of toast, Mom. I'm going to play basketball with the guys at the school, and then we'll grab a burger or hot dog. But hey, Mom, I could use some cash for lunch and whatever."

Susie got her wallet and gave Greg ten dollars. She told him that should hold him for lunch and with a little extra. Greg just looked at the money and thought, *No way in hell. This won't buy three pills.* He would just have to help himself to some of his mom's jewelry. *Honestly,* he thought, *she never wears it, and she won't notice it. When she dies, I would inherit anyway, so I'm not really stealing it. I'm just collecting my inheritance a little early.*

Greg told his mom that he was going to go up and change clothes, and instead of going into his room, he went into his parents' room and opened her jewelry box and just took her broach. He felt a little nag of guilt as he picked it up, but then he knew that he needed it more than his mom did. Susie gave Greg a hug as he left the house, and then she decided to spend the day catching up on laundry and then maybe curl up with a book. She reminded Greg to come home for dinner, and she would make something special and bake a cherry pie, his favorite. Greg ran out the door and told his mom he would try, and in his heart he did really want to try. He missed his mom and dad, and he knew what he was doing would hurt them, but he just didn't know how to stop. And he wasn't sure he wanted to.

CHAPTER 25

Joan

Joan and Bob had enjoyed a quiet Sunday, with Sandy joining them for dinner Sunday night. Bob had worked the morning at the store but had come home around two to mow the lawn and catch up on a few chores. He was in a good mood, the paint sale had done very well, and he had gained a few new customers. Being the owner of a small-town hardware store, he needed to keep his customers loyal, so they wouldn't go to the big box stores in Napa or Santa Rosa. Every new body in the store was a future customer and, ultimately, a friend. Bob liked to think of himself as an easygoing guy that made friends easily.

Once Joan was back to work on Monday, she ran into Frank in the hallway, and Frank asked her to join him for lunch in the cafeteria at noon. She was glad to accept his invitation and told him she would get there as close to noon as she could make it. Joan arrived at five after twelve and apologized to Frank, telling him she had a crazy busy morning. She was beginning to think the whole population of St. Helena had come in for emergency surgery, the flu, or broken bones. She asked Frank, "What were these people doing over the weekend that they all end up on my floor on Monday morning? I think they're conspiring against me. I feel like I'm on bedpan duty."

Frank laughed and told Joan, "That's what I love about you. You give a new meaning to medicine, and not a pretty picture I might add." Frank then told Joan that he had hung his new artwork, and it looked terrific. He liked his little rental house, and the town was beginning to feel like home. He inquired about Joan's Sunday, and she told him that after church, she had just stayed home, caught up on housework and fixed a nice meal. She signed and told Frank that her life was not very exciting: it was work, home, bocce, cooking, and back to work. She was beginning to think she was in a rut that she would never escape from.

Frank asked Joan to explain bocce. He had heard about it but had never played it. It sounded intriguing to him. So Joan spent the rest of lunch explaining the game to Frank. Frank asked Joan that if she ever had time after work, would she take him over the local courts and show him how to play? He told her that he needed a hobby and needed to meet some new people.

Joan offered to take Frank over to the courts on Wednesday evening at five. if he was free by then. "The courts should be relatively free, and we can spend an hour going over the rules before I have to run home to start dinner." She gave Frank the address, and they both agreed to meet on Wednesday night.

Frank was dressed casually in jeans when he met Joan on Wednesday evening. The weather was starting to warm up, with spring right around the corner. Joan spent ten minutes going over the rules, and then they played against each other on either end of the court. Joan was impressed that Frank caught on very quickly. A few more lessons, and he might be able to beat her or at least give her a good run. By six, Joan was ready to head home, and Frank thanked her for a great lesson and told her how much fun he'd had. He could see how a person could get addicted to the sport.

Frank asked if Joan had time to stop for a glass of wine or cup of coffee, but Joan felt she should get home. Another night, she promised, and Frank said he would hold her to it. He walked Joan to her car and gave her a quick hug before she climbed in. "Thanks for your friendship. It means a great deal to me." Joan waved to Frank as she drove off. *What a nice man he is,* she thought. *He is kind and considerate and fun to be with. Bob never has time for me anymore. All he cares about is that stupid store. It wouldn't hurt him to take time to spend with me or his kids. Even though they're almost grown, they still need their dad. I wish Bob could be just a little bit like Frank. Frank makes me feel good, feel wanted, and he treats me with respect. Oh well, no sense wishing for something that will never happen. Bob doesn't seem to care anymore.*

Joan had a nice dinner on the table when Bob got home at eight. Joan gave Bob a hug and suggested that maybe they could get away some weekend, go to a B&B in Carmel or maybe up to Lake Tahoe.

"We just need a break from our lives and a chance to be together and rekindle our romance. What do you think? You want to have a little getaway fun with me? I'll make it interesting."

Bob told Joan he would love to, but the store was very busy right now, and they had a big inventory of the store coming up. Maybe in July or sometime this summer. "I know you understand, babe, business has to come first. But you know I love you. We'll get away soon, I promise," he said and then grabbed a beer and sat down for dinner.

Well, Joan thought, that went over well. *I know Bob loves me, but I just wish he would show it once in a while.* It had been months since they'd been intimate. *Well, it is what it is, I guess. I either live with it or leave it, and at this point Bob is calling the shots, and I can't make him care.* Joan headed to bed at ten and asked Bob if he was coming up, but he told her that he wanted to finish watching a movie. Joan muttered to herself, and she headed upstairs. *Okay then, the man has spoken.*

CHAPTER 26

Barb

Barb was determined to talk to Lacey when she got home from school on Wednesday afternoon. Barb was waiting for Lacey the minute she walked in the door. She asked Rachel and Brenda to finish their homework in the kitchen, so she and Lacey could have some alone time in the living room.

Barb started out softly, not wanting to upset Lacey. "Honey, I don't know what's going on with you or what has happened. But your dad and I know something bad has either happened, or something is really bothering you. Please tell me, nothing you have done or could do would make me love you less. We always have your back, but please, please just tell me what's wrong. What's bothering you?"

Lacey just looked down at her lap, with tears rolling down her cheeks. Lacey just shook her head and said, "Mom, I wish I could talk to you, but I can't. It's nothing you can help with. You just have to trust me to deal with it, and hopefully it will all be resolved soon. I'm not doing drugs, I'm not pregnant, and I'm not flunking out of school. So if something is bothering me, and I'm not saying something is, then just trust me to deal with it. I'm almost an adult, ready to take my driver's test in a few weeks. You just need to let me deal with my own problems. Didn't you always teach us to be self-reliant, to trust our own judgment? Well, now I'm asking you to trust my judgment and trust me. Please, Mom? Please?"

Barb hesitated and then went over and pulled Lacey into her arms. "I guess I don't have a choice, my sweet girl, if you won't let me help you. But please just know. I'm here the minute you want to talk to me and take some of this load off your shoulders. Growing up is very tough. Teenage years are especially tough. I remember being teased in school after I broke my nose. My parents didn't have health insurance and couldn't afford a plastic surgeon. So I developed a bump on my nose when it healed, and the kids laughed at me, calling me a witch, and making fun of my big nose. In all honesty, I don't think my parents realized how bad the break was, but as I grew in my teen years, my nose also became more crooked. One girlfriend told me that I could actually be pretty if I had my nose fixed. When I asked my mom if I could please have my nose done, she told me that they didn't have the money, and I should be glad that I was healthy and God gave us challenges to see if we could handle them. I went through my teenage years trying to hide my nose, with big hair, and trying never to be seen from the side. The one good thing was that we had no social media then. I learned to laugh at me before someone else did. The minute I finished college, got a job as a teacher, and had decent insurance and saved some money, I got a nose job. I did it for my self-esteem, for my self-respect. I guess my message is, if someone is teasing you or bullying you, just stand up for yourself, and don't let their words hurt you. They can't take away who you are. The words may hurt, but they can't destroy you. Only you can do that. Okay, lecture over. Sorry, but we all have our share of pain. It's how we deal with it that makes the difference."

Lacey asked if she could be excused since she had homework to do. She hugged her mom and told her that she loved her and appreciated her concern, but that she would be fine. Barb just sat there with tears running down her eyes, thinking, *God I hope so*, and praying that God would watch over her.

When Jack came home from work, dinner was on the table, and the girls had finished their homework. Jack seemed in pretty good spirits, so Barb was hopeful for a pleasant evening. She wanted to talk to jack about her worries about Lacey. Once dinner was over, and the girls went up to their rooms to watch TV or text friends, Barb told Jack her concerns about Lacey and the secret that Lacey was obviously keeping to herself. Barb was convinced that Lacey was into something way over her head, and she wasn't mature enough to get out of the mess she may be in.

Jack grabbed a beer out of the fridge and told Barb to lay off the kid. That she's almost grown, she can handle her own problems. "My god, Barb," Jack said, "you treat her like a baby or a little girl. She's almost a woman. Let her figure it out for herself. You smother our girls. Just because you're a teacher, you think you know it all. Well, it's time you learned you don't know it all. Now, enough of this conversation. There's a fight on TV I want to see. Let me know if Lacey kills somebody and ends up in jail, and then I'll start to worry."

After Jack walked out, Barb started washing the dishes as her tears fell into the sink mixing with the dishwater. She knew she was in this alone. Jack wasn't going to help or even acknowledge that Lacey had a problem. *Maybe I need to see a therapist. I need a support system somewhere, and I sure as hell don't have one at home,* she thought as she finished the dishes and cleaned up the kitchen.

Upstairs, Lacey had locked herself in her room and had made a few new cuts on the inside of her arm.

She knew that cutting was bad, she had heard girls talking about it at school, and she knew she should quit; but right now, it just made her feel better, more in control. It broke her heart to think how she was hurting her mom. She knew her dad cared but not as much as her mom, and he never showed it anymore. Her dad used to take the girls to the park to play ball or go bowling, but now he was either gone, drinking, or just ignoring them. She knew her mom was unhappy, and she wanted to help her mom, but how could she when she couldn't even help herself?

The next morning, Barb vowed to call her insurance company to see if their health care would cover a psychologist or social worker to talk to. She had to find someone to share her problems and worries with. Maybe Lacey would agree to go with her. They both needed help, and she was becoming more aware that she couldn't deal with their problems alone.

Maggie

As Maggie drove to bocce Thursday night, she was determined to pull Susie aside and mention her concerns to her about Greg. If Jeff thought Greg was in trouble, then she owed it to her friend to say something. She was so grateful that Jeff was such a good kid, not giving her any problems. Michael had been a handful when he was a teenager, but now he was a responsible college student. She felt blessed that her family was in such a good place.

Bocce went great, and the team won two out of three again. They were now in third place overall in the whole league of twenty-two teams. They were kicking ass, so to speak. The four women were in great spirits when they went to their usual spot for the after-dinner drinks and conversation. The women called their get-togethers BCD night: bocce, chatting, and drinks.

Once they had sat down and placed their orders, they started sharing and filling each other in on the weekly happenings: had it been a good week? A so-so week? Or a horrid week?

"Okay," Maggie said, "who wants to start? Give us the dirt, the sex, and the secrets. I'm ready."

Joan said she would start and told the ladies about Frank—Dr. Harris—and helping him pick out artwork and having a glass of wine with him and, yes, a few lunches. Joan continued, "Before you all freak out, I just want you to know it's all harmless. We're just good friends, and he needs my help since he doesn't know anyone in town. He's just a nice guy that I like, and he's a really good doctor."

Barb laughed and told Joan that she was protesting too much. Barb also wanted to thank Joan for Sandy offering to talk to Lacey, and then she filled the ladies in on Lacey's behavior and how worried she was. She asked if any of the ladies had a professional psychologist that Barb and possibly Lacey could see?

"I called my insurance company, and they'll pay for six months of therapy, and I think it's time. I can't deal with all of this on my own anymore." Barb turned to Maggie and Joan and said, "You're both in the medical field. Do you have any recommendations?"

Joan said she knew a good psychologist that the hospital used, and she would text or e-mail Barb the woman's information. Both Maggie and Joan agreed that it sounded like Lacey needed some professional help.

Maggie then turned to Susie and said, "I was going to bring this up when we were alone or in a more private setting, but I wanted to talk to you about a rumor that I heard about Greg. I've heard that he's hanging with a bad crowd of kids, kids that are into drinking, drugs, and maybe things even worse—if there is anything worse than drugs at this age. I don't want to alarm you, but I just wanted you to be aware so that you could look into it. I care about Greg, and I don't want anything bad to happen to him."

Susie seemed shocked and told Maggie that she must be wrong, but yes, she would talk to Greg about it. She mentioned that she had tried to spend time with him over the last few weeks, but he always seemed to be busy with his friends. She had asked him why he wasn't spending more time with Jeff, but Greg had said that the two boys weren't hanging out together anymore, and she had assumed they had a falling out, over a girl or something not too serious. She didn't want to tell her friend that Greg thought Jeff was a dweeb or, even worse, gay. She didn't want to hurt Maggie, so she didn't bring that up.

Maggie, changing the subject, asked Susie if she was still seeing her young friend Jay. Susie seemed reluctant to answer, but she finally told them that she had gone on a drive with Jay over the weekend. But it had been no big deal. They had actually driven to Mendocino to check out one of the wineries in the area. Maggie thought to herself that it wasn't really a lie—they had stopped by the winery for a minute to purchase a couple of bottles of wine. She didn't think her friends would approve of her relationship with Jay.

The ladies finished their wine, and each headed home, promising to see each other for practice on Tuesday if not before. They agreed that it was time to have a dinner at one of their homes. It just seemed like all their husbands were either gone or too busy to commit, but they would try to get the guys to agree.

When Maggie got home, she decided to bring up the subject of Greg with Jeff. Maybe he had new information, or maybe the boys had made up their rift. Once she had Jeff alone, she asked Jeff if he had heard any more about Greg. Or were they hanging out together again?

Jeff told his mom, "I hate to be a tattletale, but I have heard really bad things about Greg and his buddies. They cut class, and they seem to hang out with this older guy in his late twenties who works at the local garage. I've heard rumors about drug deals. And this older guy, Frankie, is the dealer. It could be all rumors, but I tell you, Mom, something is going on with Greg. He looks like a mess, doesn't spend any time with his old friends, and his girlfriend Julie broke up with him. She told me that he didn't show up for two dates and just blew her off, so she says she's done with him. I've seen her walking around with another guy on the baseball team, Scott. Scott is a really cool guy."

Maggie asked Jeff if it would help if he talked to Greg. But Jeff just shook his head. "No, Mom, he and his buddies think I'm beneath them—a nerd, an odd duck. They only laugh at me when they pass me in the halls. I want nothing to do with Greg or those hoods. Sorry, Mom, I just can't do it."

While they were on the subject of friends, Maggie decided to jump in with Jeff and ask him if he was doing okay, and who was he hanging out with. Did he have a girl he liked? She wanted to encourage him to bring his friends over and maybe meet the girl that Jeff might be interested in. She didn't want to pry, but she honestly wanted to know about his friends and stay involved in his life.

Jeff told her that he wasn't interested in any girls at this time, and he was hanging out with the usual guys that he had known since grade school. His friends were probably nerds. If you consider a guy that has good grades, likes sports, and is respectful to others nerds, then yes, they were nerds. The only difference between him and his friends was that they had girlfriends. But of course, he didn't say all that to his mom.

Maggie grabbed Jeff's hand and said, "Honey, is there anything else you want to tell me? Is there something bothering you? There's nothing that you can't tell your dad or I. We will always have your back. We love you. Don't ever be afraid to come to us."

Jeff just gave his mom a sorrowful look, but he told her that he knew that she loved him, and he would come to her if he had any problems. But for now he was fine. How could Jeff tell his mom he was gay, if he didn't know for sure that he was gay? How do you find out if you're gay? Do you just experiment, and with whom? Do you go online on or put an ad in the personals? Did his friends suspect he was gay, and would they hate him or be afraid to hang around him? Maybe Greg was in a better place than he was. Greg was maybe into drugs, but at least he knew what he was, while Jeff was still trying to find out who and what he was. Life was so confusing, and the only one he could really talk to was his big brother, Michael. Jeff decided to give Michael a call and ask him to come home for a weekend. He really needed Michael's opinion.

Maggie told Tom her concerns about Jeff when they went upstairs to bed. Maggie told Tom, "Jeff looked so sad when we were talking. I know he's holding something back from us, something he doesn't' want to share with us or is afraid to share with us. What do you think? Will you please talk to him? Maybe he'll share with you when he won't with me. Maybe it's a guy thing. Maybe he has some questions about girls, or sex, or condoms, things that I can't help him with. Please, promise me you'll talk to him."

Tom agreed to have a father-and-son talk with Jeff, although he didn't agree with Maggie that Jeff was troubled. But if it would appease her, then he would talk to Jeff. He knew that both of his sons were real guys just as his dad was. Once they were in bed, Tom turned his back to Maggie, letting his thoughts drift back to his pleasant day at the office with Sharon. Not only was she a good dentist, but she was also darn good to look at. Tom had asked Sharon to join him for lunch on Friday when they had a half day. Tom was certainly looking forward to Friday as he drifted off to sleep.

CHAPTER 28

Susie

Susie met Jay again on Monday night at their usual spot. Jay gave Susie a hug and asked her if she was okay. He had worried that he had moved too fast on Saturday and that Susie would back away from him. He felt like he was falling in love with her, and he didn't want to scare her off.

Susie told Jay that she was fine, although she was suffering some guilt pangs. She didn't want to hurt Mark, although she seriously doubted that Mark gave a damn about her anymore. He was spending less and less time at home, and he didn't even try to make excuses for his absences. He was gone three to four nights a week, and when he was home on Saturday or Sunday, he was out of the house playing golf, or spending time with one of his male friends.

Susie had talked to Mark on Sunday and asked him to please spend some time with Greg, but Mark didn't share her concerns, and was half-hearted in his response to spending time with Greg. He had told her maybe, next weekend, he would take Greg to a sporting event in the city. He would just need to check his calendar. Susie wasn't sure what was going on with Mark; he had always been a good dad to their only son, and they had always enjoyed spending time together. She could understand him being tired of his wife but certainly not his son.

Susie told Jay that she didn't want to give him up, but she thought they should slow things down a bit and not jump into a sexual relationship right now. She needed to sort out things at home.

She didn't consider herself a cheater, an adulteress, or didn't want to think of herself in those terms. She told Jay that he should feel free to see other women, and if he didn't want to wait for her to make a decision, that would be fine too. She thought they should remain friends without benefits for the near future.

Jay pulled Susie close and said, "Susie, I am willing to wait until you're ready. I'm in no hurry and you, sweet Susie, are worth waiting for. Can we at least keep meeting once or twice a week for a glass of wine or just a quick lunch? After all, I still have lots to learn about wine making, and you are the wine-making queen in these parts. In other words, we can keep our meetings on a semiprofessional level if that eases your conscience.

Susie told Jay, "Thank you. Yes, that does make me feel better. I don't want to interrupt your life. You're single and I'm not. I don't want to spoil your chances of meeting a really nice, single woman. But I am glad that you want to continue to see me. My life would have a huge hole in it without you. As they say in the movies, I've grown accustomed to your face."

Jay laughed. "Wow, babe, do you sing too? No, I am willing to wait for you to make up your mind or cure your guilty conscience. I don't want to meet some new hot babe. From what I hear about your husband, Mark, he doesn't seem to be the loving, caring husband you deserve anyway."

Susie and Jay spent the rest of their evening together talking about work and mutual friends at the various wineries. The wine industry was a tight group, where everyone knew each other and who was producing the best wines. The vintners may be competitive, but if there was a problem—fire or an infestation—the vintners had each other's back. They were a family within a family—they could insult each other, but outsiders didn't dare criticize. That was what Susie loved most about the wine industry. There were so many wonderful wines out there, and enough business to go around.

When Susie kissed Jay good night in the parking lot, she literally had to force herself to get in her car and leave him. Once they had been intimate, it was hard to just stop with a kiss. She drove home with mixed feelings, happy that Jay still wanted to see her and maybe even loved her, but also still feeling pangs of guilt. She would have loved to talk to her friends about her dilemma, but she knew they would never understand, so at this point she had to hold her own council.

Greg came in an hour after Susie got home, well after his week-night curfew. Susie stopped Greg and said, "Hey, kiddo, you're really late for a school night. What's going on with you? I think you and I need to sit down and find out what's really happening with you. I understand from Maggie that you and Jeff are no longer friends. Jeff is a good kid, good grades, and he has always been your friend. You could do worse, you know."

Greg looked down at his feet and said, "Mom, I really don't want to get into this or put down Jeff, but everyone is calling him a fag and a loser. He just acts so goody-goody, and nobody but the geeks want to hang around him. He doesn't have a girlfriend. All the chicks think he's weird. I have friends that are much cooler. And I don't want to hurt Maggie's feelings, but my friendship with Jeff is over. Now can I go to bed? I've been at the library studying with some of the guys, I have a chemistry test in the morning, and I'm bushed."

Susie couldn't think of anything else to say, but she sincerely doubted that Greg had been at the library. Lately, she had started to mistrust anything Greg was saying. He had always been a good kid. Why was he lying now? What the hell was he into?

She wished Greg a good night, and as she climbed into bed, she decided that she needed to do a bit of snooping and maybe talk to Greg's counselor at school, or maybe spend an afternoon following him, see where he went and who he was with. Maggie had hinted that Greg was hanging out with a bad crowd, and if that were true, Susie was going to put an end to it. If Mark didn't bother coming home anymore, then she was going to have to handle this problem with Greg on her own.

In San Francisco, Mark and Kim were just falling asleep in each other's arms in Kim's apartment. Mark had been as good as his word and was introducing Kim to new clients and showing her the ropes. Kim thought to herself, *I may not love the guy, but I love the boost he is giving my career. I'll hang on to him until I don't need him anymore. A girl has to take care of herself.*

CHAPTER 29

Joan

On Saturday morning, Joan reminded Sandy that she was having lunch with Lacey. Sandy told Joan that she knew, and they were meeting at an outdoor hamburger spot, so that they would have the privacy to speak and not be overheard.

Sandy promised to handle Lacey carefully and not force the subject, but just draw Lacey out and gain her trust. Sandy asked her mom what she had planned for the day, since her dad would be at the hardware store all day. Joan told her that she had volunteered to go with Dr. Harris to Napa to a nursery to look at some indoor plants to add a little color to his kitchen and living room.

Sandy said, "Mom, you're spending a lot of time with Dr. Harris. Is there something I should know? Do I need to fill you in on men's intentions? You're such an innocent, you wouldn't recognize a man hitting on you if he did it with one of dad's hammers. I know and dad knows you can be trusted, but does Dr. Harris know you can be trusted? I'm sure there are other single nurses at the hospital that could take him plant shopping."

Joan just laughed and hugged her daughter and told her that they were just good friends. She really enjoyed Frank's company, and he listened to her, which was something that Bob never did.

"Women are allowed to have men friends, you know," she reminded Sandy. "Don't you have some men friends, Sandy, guys that you enjoy spending time with but have no romantic interest in?"

Sandy told her mom that she had a few male friends that she had no interest in, but most of those guys also had girlfriends. "I trust you, Mom. Have fun, be good, and be home by six" Sandy then headed to her bedroom to change for lunch with Lacey.

Sandy met Lacey at the outside diner, and they found a table in the picnic area and then ordered burgers and milkshakes. Sandy spent the first ten minutes telling her about her college classes, who she was dating, and then she casually led Lacey into the conversation. Sandy said, "So, Lacey, what's going on? Is something bothering you? I would be glad to listen if you want to share something that you may not want to share with your parents. I'm just here to listen. Pretend I'm your favorite cocker spaniel—I'm all ears."

Lacey hesitated for a minute and then said, "Okay, let's suppose—I'm not saying this is happening, but let's just suppose, how would you handle this hypothetical situation? A man in power is bothering this young girl, touching her and making her touch him in places that she's not comfortable with. He told her if she tells, he will hurt her family, destroy her family, and he has the power to do it. The girl is afraid to tell anyone, so she keeps her mouth shut. She tries to avoid him, but unfortunately, she can't. He has a power over her that she can't explain, but she's sure at some point it will be over. So the girl is just hanging on, waiting it out, and dealing with it the best she can. He hasn't tried to have sex with the girl, but the touching makes her uncomfortable. So I'm not saying it's me or if it's true. Maybe it's one of my friends. What would you do?"

"Oh my god, Lacey," Sandy said, "is the girl you? Are you saying that some bastard is molesting you? Touching even without sex is molestation. If it were me, I'd kick his balls in and yell until the whole frickin' town heard me. Whoever the hell this man of power is it's not okay. No one should have the power over another person's body. This man belongs in jail. Tell your friend, or if it's you, someone has to know about it, to stop this man. Even if he stops hurting you or your friend, he will find another young girl, another victim. He has to be stopped. Please tell me the truth. I will help you, and we'll stop him."

Lacey had tears in her eyes and told Sandy, "I or my friend can't tell anyone. He will ruin the family. He told my friend he would destroy them. I…umm…she needs to keep her mouth shut. Maybe he'll stop eventually, maybe it's just a temporary thing. I can't tell you anymore, so please don't ask. Don't push or I'll leave."

Sandy had no choice but to agree but told Lacey that the man wouldn't stop. It was a sickness, and he had to be put away and kept away from young girls or even young boys. "There is a name for a man like that, and it's *pedophile*, he's a pedophile. They can't be cured. He's a danger to society and should never be around young people."

Lacey made Sandy promise to not say anything to her parents or anyone. If Sandy told someone about something that Lacey told her, she would really hurt herself. Sandy had no choice, but she promised herself that she would find out who this man in power was, and she would stop him. She then suggested they eat their lunch and change the subject. She didn't want to upset Lacey any more than she already had.

They were almost finished with lunch, when Lacey pushed up her sleeve to wipe up some ketchup, when Sandy noticed the reddish slashes on Lacey's arm. Sandy grabbed Lacey's arm and asked what had happened to her arm.

"Oh," Lacey told her, "I just cut my arm helping Mom wash dishes."

Sandy said, "Lacey, I don't believe you. I think you're cutting. I read about it in one of my nursing classes. It's becoming more common in young people. They cut themselves to dull the pain of the other real pain inflicted by others or some trauma. Cutting is a serious issue, Lacey, and you need to see someone, a professional. The cutting will just get worse. I will help you deal with it, but we need to ask a professional. It can become a real sickness."

Lacey just broke into tears and ran out of the picnic area, leaving the rest of her lunch. Sandy just sat there, stunned. She knew this was serious, and she now felt obligated to help this frightened young girl. She had to get to the bottom of this and find out who this bastard was and see him in jail. She couldn't tell Lacey's parents—she had promised—but she could talk to a professional, and she could start checking on Lacey after school. She wondered if the pervert was a priest, a teacher, or even a relative or one of her parents' friends. But whoever it was, Sandy intended to find out.

Joan met Frank at his house at eleven, and they drove in Frank's car to the nursery in Napa. They had a good time just walking around the nursery looking at the options for indoor and outdoor plants. After much perusing, they chose three indoor plants—one for the kitchen and two for the living room. They were healthy varieties of philodendron. These were easy-to-care for plants only needing water, food, and a window close to give them sunlight. Frank was very pleased with their choices and told Joan that he wished he owned a home, so he could do some landscaping and plant roses and hydrangeas. He told her that he had always enjoyed working in the yard and would love a vegetable garden. When he knew he was going to stay in St. Helena, depending on his contract with the hospital, he would start looking at houses to purchase.

Frank suggested they have lunch in Yountville as a reward for their hard work. Frank also ordered a bottle of champagne to celebrate their good fortune. Joan laughed and teased Frank. "We bought plants, not a heart or lung machine." Frank clinked glasses with Joan and told her he thought they were very similar; they both give life.

Joan said, "I've got to give it to you, Frank, you're good. You've got a way with words. No wonder your patients adore you. Honesty, though, I had a great time. I always enjoy walking through the nursery, whether I buy anything or not. You're right, though, the nursery is full of life and in some ways hope. Plants reaching for the sun fighting to live, just needing the basics for survival."

Frank responded, "Now who's being poetic? No wonder I enjoy your company so much. We think alike. Honestly, Joan, I don't know what I would do without your friendship. I've never met a woman like you: beautiful, smart, and with a kind soul. Thank you for being my friend."

Joan was touched and not sure how to respond. She just told Frank, "Thank you." Joan was safe from a more serious discussion when lunch arrived, and then the conversation turned lighter with talk of their work and funny stories of their coworkers.

After a two-hour lunch, Frank drove Joan back to her car at his house. When he walked Joan to her car, he thanked her again, and then he leaned in a gave her a gentle kiss on the lips and whispered to her, "I mean it, Joan, I really care about you. And I'm beginning to feel that what's between us is more than friendship. I don't expect an answer now, but think about it. I would love to spend more time with you. I haven't felt this way about a woman in a long time, maybe never. You are precious to me. Remember that always."

Joan was frankly shocked. She really liked Frank and respected him. But did she have feelings beyond that? She wasn't sure. She touched Frank's hand and said, "I really care about you as a dear friend. But I'm not sure about more. Let's just be friends for now and see what happens. That's all I can offer for now. I'm happily married, or at least I thought I was happily married until recently. I just need time to think. Please give me time and remain my friend."

Frank told Joan that he would always be her friend. If more came of it, fine; if not, that would be fine too. He just wanted her to know how special she was to him. He told her he'd see her at the hospital on Monday, and he hoped he hadn't upset her, but he just wanted her to know where he stood.

Joan drove home deep in thought. She certainly hadn't seen that coming. She really liked Frank, maybe even more than *liked*, but his declaration had taken her by surprise. When she walked into the house deep in thought, she found Sandy sitting at the kitchen table doing her homework.

Joan asked Sandy how lunch had gone with Lacey. Had Lacey told Sandy what was bothering her? And had she shared more than she had with her parents? Sandy told her mom that she had promised Lacey that she wouldn't disclose their conversation. "But I can tell you she's in way over her head." Sandy suggested that Joan tell Barb to keep a close eye on Lacey. Sandy also said to tell Barb that Sandy was going to keep trying to help Lacey, and she was thinking of a plan to do just that.

Barb went to the refrigerator to pull out something for dinner, but her thoughts were on her afternoon spent with Frank. Sandy was also deep into her thoughts. How was she going to help Lacey? And where should she start? The only thing she knew for sure was that she would get to the bottom of this and remove this scum ball from Lacey's life.

CHAPTER 30

Barb

Barb was putting away groceries when Lacey walked into the house. Barb asked Lacey how lunch went. And did she and Sandy have a good time? How was Sandy enjoying college? Was she dating anyone special?

Lacey just turned away from her mom and said, "I really don't want to talk about it. Sandy is fine, her life is fine, she doesn't have any problems, and she's just fine. I'm going up to my room to study. Please ask the girls to leave me alone. I just need to be alone for a while."

Barb was stunned by Lacey's anger. She had never spoken to either of her parents in that tone before. *Oh my god*, she thought, *this is really serious.* Barb decided to call Joan and see what Lacey had shared with Sandy. Joan answered and told her what little that she knew from what Sandy had told her. She told her that Sandy had been sworn to secrecy, but she did pass on the info to please keep an eye on Lacey. Sandy had told her that whatever Lacey was going through was serious, and she was very vulnerable. Joan didn't know more than that, but Sandy seemed determined to help Lacey.

Barb asked Joan if it would help if she talked to Sandy, but Joan said, "I doubt it. She promised Lacey she would honor her privacy, but I do know she is going to do everything she can to help Lacey. I would suggest you keep a close eye on her, but don't push. She'll tell you what's bothering her when she's ready."

Barb thanked Joan and hung up. She was so frustrated. What could she do to help Lacey? She couldn't force Lacey to talk to her. All she could do was wait and watch, and pray. She asked Brenda to watch Rachel; she was going to go over to the Catholic church to light a candle. Maybe God would lead her in the right path. In the past when she had felt like this, her faith had always pulled her through, even the darkest times.

That night after dinner, Barb pulled Jack aside into the living room and told him what she had heard about Lacey and her lunch with Sandy. She told Jack that they had to find a way to help Lacey with whatever problem she was dealing with. She told Jack how worried she was and that she was afraid Lacey would do something stupid, something to harm herself.

Jack again just blew off Barb's concerns. He told her that she always worried too much about the girls and that she should just let them alone to deal with their own problems. He warned her to back off and stop fussing over the girls, or he would step in. His opinion was more discipline—make Lacey take on more household chores. If she was busy enough, she wouldn't have time to get so consumed in her own problems. "Now, Barb," he said, "if you'll excuse me, I have a game to watch."

Barb just sat down on the couch and put her head in hands and let the tears fall. There was no help in Jack; she would get more support from her friends than from her husband. When had he become so angry, so unsupportive of his family? He had been so great with the girls when they were little. Jack used to coach Lacey's baseball team. Was it the drinking? His job? What had changed him so completely? Was there any hope for them, or was this the end of their family?

Upstairs, Brenda tried to talk Lacey into playing board games with her and Rachel, but Lacey declined. She wasn't mean in her denial, just not interested. Lacey just wandered back to her own room as if she hadn't heard Brenda's request. Brenda and Rachel couldn't understand why their big sister was all of a sudden so distant from them, when she had always been a great big sister, playing with them, helping with homework, and "babysitting" them. Now it was like they didn't even exist.

Once Lacey was back in her own room, she pulled out the razor. She knew what she was about to do was not healthy, but she just couldn't see any other way. The little cuts really weren't hurting anyone else, so what harm was in doing it once in a while? She would stop when the other unpleasant situation stopped. Then everything would be fine, wouldn't it?

On Sunday morning, Barb took Brenda and Rachel to church with her. Lacey had refused, claiming lots of unfinished homework, and Jack never went to church. After church, Barb took the two younger girls out for lunch. She felt like she was ignoring their needs in her worry about Lacey. She felt like she was losing her entire family, and it was her fault that she was a bad mother.

When they got home, Jack had left a note that he was going to a local bar to watch a game with some of the guys, and for them not to wait at dinner for him. *Great*, Barb thought, *now I have to worry about what trouble he will get in and what will he will be like when he comes home.* Great, just stack another brick on her back, she could take it.

The rest of Sunday, Lacey stayed in her room, only coming out for dinner, and Barb played Clue with Brenda and Rachel after dinner. Barb was not going to wait up for Jack when he came staggering in.

Barb was sound asleep when Jack came home and fell over a kitchen chair. Barb went downstairs when she heard the banging and found Jack sound asleep on the kitchen floor. Fine, just fine, and she went back to bed, leaving Jack to sleep if off on the floor. The hell with him, she thought, the hell with him!

CHAPTER 31

Maggie

Maggie's week had started out busy being short-staffed at the pharmacy, which made her late getting home to start dinner and late for bocce practice. She stopped at a local deli to pick up soup and sandwiches for dinner for Jeff and Tom before she ran off to practice.

When she got home from practice, she found the soup untouched and the sandwiches still in their wrappers. *Where was everyone?* she thought. She found a note from Jeff, saying he was out with a friend at the library, but there was no note from Tom. Maybe he had a late patient, or more likely an emergency had come up. A toothache or abscess were never scheduled; they just happened. She heated up some soup for herself and bit into the sandwich, which was getting hard.

Since she had the evening to herself, she could watch some TV in peace and maybe start on the new book that she had checked out of the library. She was sure that Tom would be home soon.

Tom had closed the office right on time at five and had asked Sharon if she would like to stop somewhere for a glass of wine. He wanted to thank her for the great job she was doing and maybe talk about some new equipment that she had recommended for the office. Tom and Sharon had enjoyed a long lunch on Friday, and the more time he spent with Sharon, the more time he wanted to spend with her. She was a fascinating woman, and he really enjoyed her humor and light banter with him and the office staff. The woman could respond with humor to a young patient and sympathy with an older client. She was a woman of many talents, and those talents weren't lost on Tom.

Sharon agreed to stop for a quick glass of wine, but she was concerned that his wife might be holding dinner for him.

"Oh no," Tom assured her, "my wife has bocce practice on Tuesday nights and a bocce game on Thursday nights. So she has her own life." He continued to explain—or more like complain—that Maggie wasn't around much for him or Jeff. He made it sound like Maggie was a neglectful wife and mother. It was a common line from a married man: "My wife doesn't understand me," "She ignores me," "We have no sex life," etc.

Sharon had been around enough that she had heard that line before, but she had to admit that she had never met Maggie, nor had Maggie ever reached out to her. So maybe Tom was right and Maggie didn't care. She also had to admit that Tom was a good-looking guy, a successful dentist, and it wouldn't hurt to stay on his good side. She would like to become a full partner in his practice someday. She enjoyed St. Helena and wanted to stay in the charming little town, so what was the harm in a few lunches or glasses of wine? No big deal.

Jeff, in the meantime, had gone to the library and used the library computer to go online and look at websites to meet people and especially gays meeting other gays. He wasn't even sure if these websites existed. He also wanted to check out a few books on the subject and learn more about it. What he really needed was to talk to another gay male that could answer all his questions. His brother Michael had been supportive, but he didn't really understand what Jeff was feeling. His biggest thought was *How do I meet another gay guy my age?* Then he thought, *Maybe I should try to date another girl. Maybe I didn't try hard enough. Maybe the last girl wasn't right for me. Maybe I should go to a professional.* That sounded reasonable to him. He had heard some of the guys at school talk about a place up the valley that had women who would have sex for money. Then he would know for sure if he liked girls or not, and no one would know. The women were pros and would guard his secrecy. The more he thought about it, the more the idea seemed perfect. Now he just needed to find out where it was and how much it would cost. He went home from the library feeling better—he had made a decision and a way to move forward and would find out for sure.

When Jeff got home, he found his mom curled up on the couch watching an old black-and-white movie.

"Hi, Mom," Jeff said, "where's Dad? I thought you'd both be home by now." Maggie told Jeff that she thought his Dad must have had an emergency and that there was soup and stale sandwiches in the kitchen. She asked Jeff how the library was, and what paper was he working on for school. She offered to help him if he would like or needed help. But Jeff just smiled back at his mom and told her it was research on a science project, and he had it under control. He then went into the kitchen to heat up the soup and make a peanut butter sandwich.

Jeff hated to lie to his mom, but it really wasn't a lie, was it? It was kind of a science project, and he thought he had it under control. There was no sense worrying his parents until he knew for sure if he was or wasn't gay. He had heard of gaydar, but obviously his wasn't working yet, or maybe he just needed to find the right channel.

When Tom got home at nine thirty, Maggie was heading up to bed, and Jeff had already retreated to his room. Maggie gave Tom a smile and said to him, "That must have been one hell of a toothache to keep you at the office so late. Is the patient okay? Will I have prescriptions to fill for antibiotics or pain pills in the morning for the poor soul?"

Tom looked at Maggie like she was nuts, and then he realized she thought he had worked late with an emergency. *This is a better excuse that I was going to give,* he thought. He told Maggie that the poor guy had an abscess, but he had given him some antibiotics and painkillers that he kept at the office, so his patient should be fine. He mentioned that the guy would need a crown once the infection cleared up. Tom told Maggie he was bushed and was heading to bed. He was anxious to get in the shower. He didn't want Maggie picking up the scent of Sharon's perfume on his body. Even though he hadn't kissed her, he had held her hand and given her a hug and, well, a guy can't be too careful. No sense giving Maggie something to nag him about; he knew she could be obsessive and jump to the wrong conclusions.

Once Jeff was in his room, he called one of his best friends and asked him if he knew of or if he could find out about the location of a house "Where...uh...hookers worked."

His friend said, "Wow, man, it's about time. I was beginning to think you might have a problem with...uh...you know, girls. Glad to hear you're one of us. Yeah, I know where the place is. I'll bring the address to school tomorrow. Honestly, it's the best way to learn the ropes. These gals are pros, you're gonna love it."

CHAPTER 32

Susie

Susie got to bocce Thursday night twenty minutes early, so she could practice a bit before the game started. She had been late for practice on Tuesday night, so she needed to be ready for tonight's game. She had worked late Tuesday night to make up for quitting work early on Monday night to be with Jay. She was beginning to feel like she was running on a hamster wheel, always playing catch up. She was trying to split her time with work, bocce, Greg, and Mark if he was around. Which he wasn't most of the time.

The team won all three games this time and were in a very jovial mood when they went for their usual wine night. Susie suggested a new Cabernet Franc that her winery had made, and she ordered four glasses once the women agreed to give it a try. Joan took a sip and pronounced it yummy. She said she could easily become addicted to this. She asked Susie how much a bottle the wine sold for, and once Susie told her, Joan told the others, "Well, that addiction didn't last long. I can't afford the really good stuff. I guess I'm back to Trader Joe's Two-Buck Chuck." The others laughed, and Susie told her that she could get Joan a discount if she really liked it, or maybe for a special occasion. Susie would keep this in mind and give Joan a half a case for her birthday.

The subject quickly changed to other things and how their lives were going. Maggie asked Barb how Lacey was doing, if she had told her parents what her problem was. "No," Barb told them, "but Sandy has been talking to her, and I believe that if anybody can get through to Lacey, it would be Sandy."

Joan said she had to agree, that her daughter seemed to have found a cause, and that cause was Lacey. And when Sandy has a cause, she doesn't give up. She thanked Barb for her faith in her daughter and told her that she too had to keep the faith.

Susie suggested that the ladies and their husbands come to her house for dinner Saturday night. "We can barbecue steaks and chicken and just make it a simple, casual meal." The other women could bring sides if they wanted, and they could play bridge, charades, or board games after. Susie told them that she would provide the wine, maybe not the Franc, but something good nonetheless. If the husbands want beer or something stronger, the guys can BYOB.

Maggie thought that sounded great; she would talk to Tom, but yes count them in. She would bring a big salad and garlic bread. Barb also agreed that it would be fun and offered to bring au gratin potatoes. Barb was a little worried about bringing Jack, though; she never knew how he would behave when alcohol was involved.

Joan said count her in, if she could drag Bob out of that damn store. She offered to bring dessert. Susie said, "Well, now that's settled. Joan, what is going on with Bob and that damn store? Does he prefer the store knobs to your knobs? Sorry, bad joke. Seriously, is he spending more time at work than he is at home? What do you think is going on? Is the store having problems?"

Joan told Susie that no, the business had been doing well, maybe too well. "He thinks he has to be at the store every hour that it's open. He doesn't trust the staff to do their jobs." She said she saw Sandy more than Bob. Joan honestly thought that Bob was trying to avoid her by staying away so much. She told them that she had suggested they go away for a weekend, and he had turned her down. He always told her later, next week, next month, next year. She was getting tired of the next that never happened.

Maggie told them that she was going through the same thing, that Tom was spending more time at the office than he used to. She thought his bringing in another dentist would give him more free time, not less. "Whoa," Susie said, "have you seen this new dentist that Tom brought into the practice? Is she pretty? Single? How old? Give us the dirt."

Maggie told them that she had not met Dr. Sharon Nelson yet. She had suggested to Tom that he invite Sharon to the house for dinner, but Tom had just blown her off and changed the subject. Maggie knew Sharon was single, but that was all she knew about her.

Susie said, "Brainstorm. Let's invite Sharon and a date or alone to join us for dinner Saturday night, and we can check her out. If she doesn't have a date, I can find one of the guys at the winery to join us."

Barb laughed and suggested Jay. "He's single and a cutie. What about Jay? Speaking of Jay, Susie, what's going on with you and Jay?"

Susie told them she didn't think that was such a good idea. She really didn't want him on her home turf. She thought to herself, she wasn't into sharing, and Jay was hers. She just told them that she didn't think they would have much in common, and she really didn't want Jay that close to her husband. Not that there was anything between her and Jay but friendship, but still it would be awkward.

Maggie said she would ask Tom to invite Sharon, and she would let Susie know if Sharon would bring a date or if Susie needed to find a man to fill in. They didn't want to make Sharon feel like the odd man out. The women all agreed that Saturday night sounded perfect, and they would let Susie know on Friday morning if their husbands were available.

Susie kind of sidestepped the questions about Jay, and the subject soon changed to their children and other topics. Susie headed home with a pizza that she had ordered for their dinner. She wasn't sure if Mark was going to be home tonight, but Greg loved pizza, so she knew he would appreciate the effort. Maybe the two of them could sit down and have a little talk; she had really been worried about him. He had been so remote lately, and she thought he seemed jittery and nervous. She worried that maybe he was ill or, God forbid, gotten involved in drugs.

When she walked into the house, it was empty. Greg was gone and so was Mark. *Fine*, she thought, *I have the pizza all to myself.* She could heat up the pizza when Greg got home. She fixed herself a slice and sat down to watch the news and wait up for Greg. She would wait up all night if she had to, but she was going to talk to Greg. He had been ignoring curfew way too often. If Mark wouldn't deal with Greg, she would. Somebody needed to be a parent in this house.

While Susie was home worrying about Greg, Greg was out with his new buddies at the bowling alley playing video games. The boys had met with their friend Frankie from the garage earlier and gotten their stash of drugs. They divided up the drugs depending on how much money each had contributed. Greg had hocked his mother's broach, but the money was almost gone. Greg hadn't realized that being part of this gang of guys was going to be so expensive.

Greg told the guys that he was having a hard time coming up with all that cash, and could he pay for his share the next time? But no, the guys told him, no cash, no stash. Okay, Greg, agreed he would come up with the money and get his share when they met next Monday night. He would just have to deal with the small amount he had for the next few days, or he could try to do without them. How bad could it be?

When Greg got home, his mom was sound asleep on the couch. He had escaped another cross-examination. His mom was starting to really get on his nerves, always bugging him, asking where he had been, who he had been with, and trying to get him to hang out with dorky Jeff. He had new friends that had visions, and they knew how to have fun. Greg snuck into his mom's room and quietly opened her jewelry box and pulled out a ring that had been her grandmother's. It's not like she ever wore the darn thing, he thought, she always said it was too big for her, and she never got around to having it sized her. This was an emerald ring and should give him enough cash for the next month or so.

Greg went to bed feeling better about his situation. He could hang on until Monday with the few pills he had left. It wasn't like he was an addict. He could do without the drugs; he just liked the high. But he didn't need them; no, he wasn't like some of the guys.

When Susie woke up on the couch, it was early on Friday morning. She went to check on Greg, and he was sound asleep in his bed. The little rat, she thought, he had snuck in when she was asleep. He looked so peaceful, just like he used to when he was a baby or a little boy. She could envision him holding his teddy bear. She would talk to Greg later. She knew she had to be wrong; Greg would never be mixed up with drugs. Maybe his new friends weren't as bad as Jeff had said they were. Maybe Jeff was jealous that Greg was so popular. That must be it; jealousy is such an evil thing, especially in the teen years.

Susie then went to her bed to get a few more hours' sleep before she had to get up for work. She was anxious to hear from her friends, and hopefully everybody would come to dinner on Saturday night. She knew Mark enjoyed some of the men, and it would be like old times when they all used to get together.

CHAPTER 33

Joan

Joan and Bob were running late getting to Susie's house on Saturday night. Bob had worked late at the store and got home just in time to shower and change. Joan was frustrated with Bob and told him so as they drove to Susie's. She told him that she thought he cared more about the store than her and the kids. When was the last time he had seen Brad or spent time with Sandy? She hated to have to remind him that his first obligation should be to his wife and kids. She was still concerned about Brad having bought a motorcycle. But Bob just brushed off Joan as a worrier, and he promised to try to spend more time with her and the kids.

"I know, Joan, I know. I'm not as considerate as your good buddy, Dr. Frank. I don't take you out to lunch or invite you shopping. If you want a guy like that, then you should have married someone like Frank. I'm just a normal guy trying to support my family and keep the wolves from the door. The store is doing well now, but do you know how hard I have to work to compete with the big box stores? They're cheaper and carry more stock than I can. You need to think about my situation and put yourself in my shoes once in a while. I will be a good, loving husband tonight and put on a good show for your friends, but I'm not staying late. I have to be at the store early tomorrow."

Joan just threw up her hands and told Bob that he just didn't get it. She asked him, "What happened to the man I married? The kind, considerate guy that couldn't do enough for me? Now you can't even make it in time to have dinner with us. I feel like I'm single—I eat alone, go to bed alone, and I feel very alone."

Bob just gave Joan a disdainful look and told her, "You'd better learn to live with it, or you would find yourself alone. Now put on a good face because we'll be at Susie's in a minute."

Barb warned Jack to behave when they were on their way to Susie's house. "Please just have one or two beers or glasses of wine, and no more. I don't want to be embarrassed in front of my friends, and you shouldn't want to embarrass yourself. You live and work in this town. You don't want to make a fool of yourself or be known as the town drunk."

Jack told Barb to lay off, or he would turn around and go home, and she could go by herself. He told her he was sick of her nagging, and he didn't drink any more than the other husbands. *Yeah right*, she thought, *only if the other husbands were fish.*

Barb had arranged for the girls to order pizza and watch movies. Lacey had promised to keep an eye on her little sisters. Barb was hoping a night out might be good for her and Jack, and for the girls too. If Lacey hung out with her sisters, she might relax a bit and have fun with them as she always had in the past. Brenda had always looked up to Lacey and emulated everything Lacey said, wore, or ate. Her big sister was her hero. Maybe some of this adulation would make Lacey feel more needed and more loved, and she would start to realize what she had been missing when she was in her dark moods.

Both Maggie's and Susie's husbands had agreed to the last-minute Saturday invitation, although grudgingly, but at least they would all be there. Well, Dr. Sharon would not be there. Tom had firmly said no; he did not want to encourage socializing outside of the workplace. Maggie had told Joan she thought that was odd, but she wasn't going to push it.

Susie welcomed the couples as they arrived with a big hug and took their dishes into the kitchen. She set up a table with appetizers and beer and wine. There were a bottle of bourbon, vodka, and scotch, if her guests chose anything stronger. She told them that Mark was in the backyard getting the grill ready. "So please help yourself to something to drink and nibble on, and feel free to join Mark in the yard. Dinner would be in about an hour." The three men at once had a drink in hand and went out onto the patio to join Mark.

The four women went into the kitchen to hang out with Susie as she put the finishing touches on dinner and laid out plates and napkins. Joan asked Susie, "So what's happening with you and Jay? Tell us all. Give us the scoop. I could use some fun in my life."

Susie whispered, "Shhh…the walls have ears. Or maybe Mark bugged the house." She told them again that she and Jay were just friends, and she was trying to keep it that way. Susie changed the subject quickly and asked Joan how things were going with Dr. Frank.

"Are you still taking him shopping or helping him with his garden? Anything else you have planned with Frank? Grocery shopping, picking out a new wardrobe? Do you think that he is inventing all of these errands just to see you and spend time with you?"

"No, absolutely not," Joan answered. "He's just a kind man who is lonely and getting used to a new town. I'm sure anyone of you would do the same thing. He has never been anything but a gentleman. It's nice to have a real conversation with a man who is not hurrying out the door, or is too busy to even talk to me and his children."

Maggie said, "Do I hear trouble in paradise? Are you and Bob having problems? I'm beginning to think it's a midlife-crisis thing. Tom ignores me most of the time too. I am beginning to believe in the seven-year itch, or fifteen-year itch, or whatever itch. Why do men stop caring about their wives, stop bringing us flowers, stop telling us how pretty we are?"

Barb agreed with Maggie. "Men are so nice when you meet them and when you're dating. And then the minute you marry them, they become a different person. If I knew then what I know now, I would never have married Jack. I'm so glad I have my girls, but maybe I would have had them with someone else. I don't know, sometimes I just hate him, or hate what he's become."

Joan gave Barb a hug and told her that she'd never heard her talk like that. Barb was normally such a positive person. The kids in her class loved her. Maybe Barb was just down because she was so worried about Lacey. *Maybe all of them are having husband problems, not just me*, Joan thought. *Bob is a good guy, but lately he is just so distant.*

Maybe Maggie was right. It's a guy thing where after being married for a few years, they lose interest. It doesn't mean that they don't love us, but we're just not as exciting as we used to be.

While the gals were in the kitchen, the men were on the patio enjoying their drinks and talking with Mark while he put the meat on the grill. Tom told Mark that he hadn't seen him on the golf course lately and wondered if he had been traveling for work. Mark told Tom that yes, he had been busier lately and had started doing more traveling for clients. Tom told Mark to let him know when he had some free time, and they would set up tee time. "You know, Mark, you should think about getting an assistant. If business is that good, you could use the help."

Mark said, "Actually, I did promote my new secretary, Kim, and she's been doing a great job. And she's single, so she's free to travel. The male clients love her. She's great to look at, as well as being smart of course."

Tom gave Mark a bemused look and asked if Kim was traveling with him. Mark told him, "Yeah, sometimes, but it's no big deal." Tom then asked Mark if Susie knew that Kim was traveling with him.

"No," Mark said, "and I don't think she needs to know. It's not a big deal, but I don't want her to be jealous, you know how women can be." Mark quickly changed the subject and asked Tom how his new dentist was working out.

Tom said, "Probably as well as your new secretary, Kim. He told Mark that Sharon was doing a great job, and yes, she was also pleasant to look at. Tom thought they were both lucky to have two beautiful women in their lives. Both men laughed and agreed that the wives didn't need to know, no sense in rocking their boats.

Jack and Bob were sitting on lounge chairs and discussing the Giants' lineup for the season. Jack was already on his fourth beer and starting to slur his words. Bob looked closely at Jack and asked him if he was okay, and maybe he should slow down a little bit on the beer. Bob said, "Hey, it's none of my business, but I don't want Barb to get upset with you. Joan would have my ass if I ever drank too much and embarrassed her. Actually, Joan is on my ass most of the time for working too many hours. Not spending enough time with her and Sandy, letting Brad get a motorcycle even though he's an adult. So basically, I'm a lousy husband. God, wives can be so difficult. Do you think it's a woman thing? Menopause or a midlife crisis? Joan wants constant attention, wants to go away for a weekend, thinks we need more bonding time. Doesn't she realize I have a business to run? Employees to care about? I don't get it sometimes. I just want to tell her to get the hell off my back."

Jack totally agreed. Barb was always on his case about his drinking, working late, not spending enough time with the girls. And her constant worry about Lacey was driving him crazy. Why couldn't she just let the girls be and let them grow up without her constant nagging and worrying? Just because she was a teacher, it didn't mean that she knew everything about raising children.

Susie called out and asked if the meat was ready because dinner was ready. Mark told Susie that the meat was ready, and the guys helped him carry the meat trays inside and place them on the table.

Dinner started out pleasantly, and everyone agreed that the food was delicious. The conversation was light and humorous until Mark brought up the subject of local politics and the upcoming election for town council. Tom jumped in with his thoughts for the best candidate and the pros and cons of each.

Everyone at the table contributed their thoughts of what they heard and read on each candidate. The banter stayed light and funny as each dinner guest contributed to the conversation. Then Jack jumped in with his thoughts in a less-than-gentle or conversational way. His voice got louder and louder as he disagreed with everyone at the table. He thought the candidate that most of the others liked was a pompous, overeducated ass. When Barb put her hand on his arm and tried to calm him down, his voice just got louder, and he pulled his arm away. He then proceeded to tell everyone at the table that if they voted for their candidate, they would be pompous jerks too! Jack was getting out of hand, and his behavior was obnoxious.

Bob reached over and said, "Hey, buddy, calm down. It's just a local election, and everybody should be free to voice their opinions. Let's change the subject and talk about something else. How about those Giants, huh? Think they'll make it to the World Series?"

Poor Barb was humiliated. She knew that every time Jack drank too much, he became opinionated, obnoxious, and just a jerk. This was why she hated to take him anywhere. Jack became the expert on all subjects, and if others didn't agree, he would argue it to death until everyone just gave up and walked out.

Both Tom and Mark jumped in and told Jack to calm down and not ruin the evening and the nice meal that the girls had planned. Of course, this just made Jack madder, and he told them to calm down. That he would talk about what he wanted to whenever he wanted to, and if they didn't like it, too bad. He went on to say that the others were just too stupid to understand and willing to hear his side. Then Jack jumped up from the table and went outside, opened another beer, and lay down on a patio lounge chair.

Barb apologized and asked everyone to please finish their dinner, and she didn't know why Jack was so crazy sometimes. Mark said, "Sorry, Barb, but we all know why he acts this crazy. It's because he drinks too much. This is not the first time that he's made an ass of himself. He needs therapy or to go into treatment."

Tom and Bob both agreed but not as vigorously as Mark had done. Both felt so sorry for Barb; she was a good woman and didn't deserve this kind of behavior. The others tried to finish their dinner and change the subject, but by this time the mood had been ruined. As soon as dinner was over, the women went into the kitchen to help Susie clean up, and then the men went into the living room to share cigars and talk sports. Tom pulled Bob aside and asked Bob if he had noticed Jack's behavior worsening since he often went fishing with him.

Bob hesitated and then told Tom that, yeah, sometimes when they went fishing even early in the morning, Jack would bring beer and would finish a six-pack by noon. Bob told him that he always drove and picked up Jack, but they hadn't gone fishing for months since Bob had been so busy with the store.

Everyone decided to call it an early night since the mood had been ruined. Bob offered to help Barb load Jack into the back seat of Barb's car, since Jack was now out cold in the backyard. Between Bob and Tom, they were able to drag Jack out and lay him out on the back seat. The women gave Barb a hug and told her to hang in there, that they all loved her.

Joan pulled Barb aside and told her to call if she needed anything. She said that she knew of a good rehab program in Calistoga, and she would be glad to check into it for Barb. She reminded Barb that alcoholism was a disease and nothing to be ashamed of. But she agreed that Jack needed professional help.

The others soon departed after Joan drove off after thanking Susie and Mark for a wonderful dinner. *Yeah right,* Susie thought, *another exciting night in small-town America.* At least Greg wasn't home to witness their friend's humiliation. Mark told Susie that he was going to bed. His heart couldn't take all this excitement, and he had an early tee time the next day.

When Barb got home, she pulled the car into the driveway and went into the house in tears. She left Jack to sleep it off in the car. If he froze his ass off, so much the better, she thought. How much more could she take? She was constantly worried about Lacey, and Jack's horrible behavior was just one more weight on her back. She knew she needed to find a professional to talk to. Joan had suggested a name of a good therapist at the hospital, and Barb was going to call her on Monday. If any family needed help, it was theirs.

Joan told Bob on their way home how sorry for Barb she was and what a miserable life she was leading with a drunken husband and a daughter in crisis. Joan then proceeded to tell Bob what she had heard about Lacey's problems. Bob agreed that Jack needed professional help and possibly Lacey too. He also told Joan that she was not just a good nurse but also a good person.

Joan was stunned. A compliment from her husband—she couldn't believe it. What was this world coming to? Instead, she thanked Bob and told him that they needed to treasure what they had, because life could change in the blink of an eye. She told him of some of the heartbreaking stories she saw at the hospital. She reached over and hugged him and said, "Life is precious, Bob, and we need to hold it like a precious jewel and continue to shine it. Otherwise, it will be tarnished." She held Bob's hand as they drove home. She felt closer to him than she had in months.

CHAPTER 34

Barb

Sunday morning, as Barb was fixing pancakes for the girls, Jack wandered into the kitchen and asked Barb to fix him some coffee and breakfast. He wanted to know why Barb had left him in the car all night. He complained that his back ached, and he thought he was coming down with a cold. Why Hadn't Barb woken him up when they got home?

She told him she didn't want to discuss it in front of the girls, but if he would go into the living room, she would be glad to tell him about the wonderful show he had put on Saturday night at Susie's house. Once they sat down in the living room, Barb gave him the look and let loose with her disgust and told him that he had made an ass out of himself last night, getting drunk, arguing with everyone at the table, and basically picking a fight with everyone. She went on to say that she didn't know how she would face her friends at bocce. He had made a fool of himself and her by his disgusting display of drunkenness. She said "I'm going to give you one more chance to get professional help, or I'm done. I heard about a really good rehab center in Calistoga, and I'll check, but I think our health insurance will cover it. Jack, I can't go on like this anymore. It's not good for the girls or me. I have enough to worry about with Lacey without you acting like a fourth child."

Jack gave Barb a cold look and responded, "I'm not going anywhere. Rehab is for alcoholics, and I'm not one, so forget it. I had a few too many beers, no big deal. I'm not the first person that your fancy friends have seen drunk. As far as the conversation at the table, it was a friendly discussion. I was sharing my opinion and was inviting their opinions. Just because these people have a burr up their ass doesn't mean they don't have an opinion now and then. Although sometimes I wonder. You just overreacted. I'm sure no one thought a thing about it but you. No one probably even noticed."

"Really? Really? No one noticed?" Joan replied. "Bob helped me drag your body out to the car. Everyone noticed and felt pity for me and lost any respect they may have had for you. You made a scene, a fool of yourself. I doubt we'll be invited anywhere again by my friends."

Jack told Barb that he could care less if he was ever in their company again. He thought they were all snobs, and the only decent guy in the group was Bob, and sometimes that was questionable. He also told Barb to get off his back. He would live his life the way he wanted, and if she didn't like it, she could just pack up and leave and take the girls with her. He was sick of her always smothering the girls, the constant worrying about them. He thought Lacey was just fine and just rebelling against her mother. He added that if she left, he would not support her or the girls, and she would come crawling back. "So, Barb," he said, "get off your high horse and off my back. And start being the woman I married and not the nagging bitch you've become. I'm damn tired of your behavior, so you better shape up, or I'll ship out." He laughed at his own joke and walked out of the house.

Barb just sad down on the couch and cried. What in the hell was she supposed to do now? She knew Jack would never get help until he realized that he needed help. How do you get someone to admit that they're an alcoholic? She knew that if Jack wouldn't get help, she would have to. She remembered that Joan told her about a therapist at the hospital that took private patients for counseling. She knew that she couldn't help Lacey or Jack if she couldn't help herself. She had to admit she was lost, in over her head, and she couldn't see a clear path out.

She was too embarrassed to call Joan, so she sent Joan a text, thanking her for her and Bob's help last night, and asking for the name of the therapist that Joan recommended. A few minutes later, Joan sent over the name and phone number of the therapist. She also told Barb that there was no need to thank her or Bob for their help. She told Barb that she loved her and would always have her back. She was just sorry that Barb had to put up with Jack's behavior, but maybe someday he would see the light and straighten up. But in the meantime, Barb had to take care of the girls and herself.

Rachel and Brenda came into the living room and sat down on either side of Barb and gave her a hug. Rachel said, "Please don't cry, Mom. Dad didn't mean to hurt your feelings. He just doesn't seem like the dad he used to be. Why has he changed so much, Mom? Was it us? Did we do something wrong to make him mad? Is it because of Lacey that he's being so mean?"

Barb just pulled the girls close and told them no, it was not their fault or Lacey's fault. She tried to explain that their dad drank too much sometimes, which changed his personality. And at this time he wasn't willing to stop drinking or change, so they would just have to keep doing the best they could. And maybe do more things without Dad. She didn't want them to stop loving him, but she also didn't want to expose them to his angry moods and drunken behavior. She also told the girls that she was going to see a therapist, a person that she could talk to that might be able to help her with the problems with Jack and Lacey too. She told the girls that sometimes a person's load gets too heavy, and they need to ask another person to share that load, or maybe give them the advice on how to lighten the load. Brenda totally understood what her mother was saying, and Rachel thought it sounded good for her mother to find someone to make her feel better.

Barb suggested that she and all three girls go to the movies, since it was obvious that Jack would be gone all day. Brenda and Rachel both jumped at the chance, but Lacey declined, saying she had too much homework, and there was a movie on Lifetime that she wanted to watch. Lacey gave her mom a hug and told her not to worry, that things would work out. She did say something that did bother Barb: Lacey asked Barb why all men were so unkind and selfish, thinking about their own sick needs and having no respect for women or their bodies.

Barb said, "What do you mean, Lacey? Has some man bothered you, or has Dad said or done something bad to you?"

"No," Lacey told her, "I was just generalizing, don't worry about it."

Lacey then headed back upstairs to her room, while her sisters and mom left for the show. That night, when Jack came home long after dinner was over and the dishes were done, he was staggering and slurring his words. He found Barb sitting at the kitchen table making a grocery list. He told Barb to fix him some dinner and asked why they hadn't waited dinner for him. Barb told him that it was after nine, and she had held dinner until seven, but the girls had school tomorrow—they had to eat and get to bed. She offered to reheat what was left of the meatloaf; it was easier just to accommodate him and reheat dinner than to get into another fight with him.

She had decided that, for the time being, it was easier just to keep silent and keep the peace until she had a chance to talk to the therapist. She would call first thing Monday morning to make an appointment with Sally Andrews, the therapist that Joan had recommended. She was really looking forward to meeting with Sally and found herself counting on the lifeline that Sally could offer.

Lacey had spent Sunday afternoon in her room watching TV and trying to talk herself out of reaching for the razor. She knew that what she was doing was harmful and unhealthy, and that cutting was not normal behavior. She finally gave in after dinner and made one small cut on her thigh. She thought that maybe she could just withdraw slowly like quitting smoking, cutting less and less until the desire was gone. She felt better after making that decision and was able to finally fall asleep.

Barb called Dr. Andrews Monday morning and made an appointment for five on Wednesday night, which was the soonest Dr. Andrews could fit her in. Dr. Andrews kept an office in town as well as being on staff at the hospital. Barb had been assured that her insurance would cover most of the office visits with a small copay that Barb could handle.

When Barb went to bocce practice on Tuesday night, she thanked Joan for the recommendation of Dr. Andrews and apologized to Susie, Maggie, and Joan for Jack's terrible behavior on Saturday night. She told the women that she had confronted Jack about his drinking, and when he had declined any help and denied his drinking problem, Barb had decided to see the therapist that Joan had recommended. She said that she felt better already just having made that decision.

The three women all gave Barb a hug and each explained that they loved her, and no apologies were needed. Susie said that she had been thinking about seeing a therapist about Greg and the sudden change in his attitude. She wasn't sure if it was just teenage boy stuff or something more serious. She laughed and said, "I wonder if she gives group rates for friends, you know, like family rates. A little therapy wouldn't hurt any of us. My husband and I don't even talk anymore about Greg or anything else. Let me know how it goes, Barb, and I may give her a call."

"Okay, ladies, Maggie called the others over to the court. Time to practice. The team we're playing Thursday night is in second place, and I hear they are tough. So get your buns over here and throw a few balls." Maggie thought it was time to lighten the mood. The conversation had been getting way too serious.

CHAPTER 35

Maggie

Maggie got home from bocce practice to find that Jeff had left a note that he was at a friend's house and would be home by ten. Tom walked in not long after Maggie, and when Maggie offered to fix Tom a late dinner, he told her that he had picked something up on the way home, and he was fine. What Tom didn't tell Maggie was that he and Sharon had stopped for a glass of wine and a hamburger. It was all innocent, but he wasn't sure Maggie would like it, so he decided not to bring it up. It had been Sharon that had invited him, saying that she hated going home to an empty house, and asked if Tom wanted to join her. He enjoyed her company, so he didn't see any harm in that, and he knew Maggie would be at bocce practice.

Maggie told Tom she was going to make herself a cup of soup and sandwich, watch the news, and wait up for Jeff. Maggie was worried about Jeff and thought maybe they should have a little heart-to-heart chat. She didn't want to push, but if Jeff was having trouble with friends or school, she wanted to know about it.

Jeff had driven to Calistoga to have a visit with the professional lady that might be able to help him with his problem and give him the answer—was he gay or not? Jeff was so nervous when he arrived at the address that he had been given. It looked like a normal Victorian house, no signs indicating what went on inside. Was he at the right place? He knocked on the door, and a very nice young woman opened the door and invited Jeff inside. She offered him a

Coke or a cup of coffee and asked if he wanted to chat first, or would he like to get started?

Jeff wasn't sure what getting started meant, but he declined the refreshment offer and explained that he was nervous, and he really didn't know how to explain his problems. The young woman told Jeff that her name was Sarah, and whatever Jeff told her was completely private, and she would never disclose their conversations.

"Please, Jeff," Sarah, said, "tell me what's bothering you. I have worked with lots of young men, even teenagers. And I am glad to help."

Jeff thanked her and told her that he did feel better, and then he explained that he wasn't sure he was attracted to girls or to guys. He felt that this indecision was making him ill, and he couldn't concentrate on his schoolwork. And some of the guys were also teasing and bullying him. He said, "Sarah, I just need to know if I'm a weirdo or not. Please help me."

Sarah took Jeff by the hand and led him upstairs to a bedroom where they would have privacy. Sarah explained her fee schedule and that she would never do more than Jeff would be comfortable with. Sarah then proceeded to get undressed and asked Jeff to do the same.

Sarah was gentle and considerate in her attempts to gain Jeff's trust and also hoped he would enjoy his first foray into lovemaking. After an hour, Sarah asked Jeff if he had enjoyed himself at all. And did he have any questions? Jeff told Sarah that it had been nice but not earthshaking, and he really didn't feel a real desire for her.

Sarah thought about it for a minute, and then she told Jeff that she would like him to come back next week. She would make an appointment with him for a young man that often worked for them. He would also be very gentle and kind, but maybe this would give Jeff the answer he needed. The young man, Joey, was very experienced and would use caution and protection. But if Jeff was going to be involved in a gay relationship, he needed to learn the ropes from a pro and learn how to be safe and smart—not be used be some inexperienced schoolboy or, worse, by an older perverted man. Jeff agreed and made an appointment with Sarah to come back the following Tuesday. He thanked Sarah for her kindness, and he had to admit that he felt better—at least he was trying to find out for himself if he was gay. Sarah had been gentle and enticing, but he had to admit that he had not found it exciting.

When Jeff got home, he found his mom lying on the couch, watching a TV movie. As soon as he walked into the room, Maggie got up and asked Jeff how his evening had gone and what he and his friends had been doing. It was kind of late to be out on a school night. Jeff told Maggie that he had met a new friend, Sarah, and they had just been chatting for a couple of hours. He told her he was sorry he was late and hoped she hadn't been worried.

"No, honey," Maggie said, "I wasn't worried, and I'm glad that you've met a new friend. You'll have to bring her by the house one of these days for dinner or just to hang out with you. Jeff told Maggie that that would be great, and he'd think about it. He said good night and headed off to bed. When he got to his room and lay down on his bed, he laughed to himself. He knew that, as nice as Sarah was, his parents wouldn't really appreciate having Sarah in their home. Especially if they knew she was a hooker.

Downstairs, Maggie was smiling to herself, glad that Jeff was making new friends, especially a girl. And maybe he was getting over his funk. The teenage years can be so difficult. She remembered back to her teenage years when every boy might be the one, every date crucial. Never say the wrong thing, never appear too eager, and never call a boy. She still remembered her mother telling her only to eat salads when on a date. "Maggie, honey," her mother had said, "you don't want to look like a glutton or have the boy spend too much money on you. And you certainly don't want to spill on your clothes. Always act like a lady and keep your legs crossed."

Her mother had been a great mom and a good person, but she was a product of the sixties. Always let the boy think that he is smarter than you, a better athlete than you. Remember, you are a lady, and ladies set limits. Why buy the cow when you can get the milk for free? *My god*, Maggie thought, *my mom was hilarious. Please, God, don't let me turn into my mother.*

Susie

Susie agreed to meet Jay on Friday night at their usual spot. They had met on Monday night, but Jay called Susie and told her how much he missed her and could she please spend a little time with him on Friday night? Susie called Mark, and he told her he was staying in the city for a late meeting and would come home on Saturday morning. Susie checked with Greg, and he was planning on being out with his friends, so she might as well have a nice evening with Jay.

Jay gave Susie a big hug as she sat down, and they ordered drinks and fish and chips. Jay told Susie, sorry, but all he could think about this week was Susie and how much he missed her. He asked if they could maybe get together twice a week or at least more often when Susie could spare it.

Susie told Jay how worried she had been about Greg and if he was involved in drugs. She told him about Greg's grades slipping, his long absences from home, and how jittery and on edge he seemed to be at times. She asked Jay what he thought about it. He was younger and hipper than she was, and maybe he knew more about the drug scene in St. Helena than she did. She didn't even know if there were illegal drugs in their small town.

Jay told her that he could certainly understand her concern, and he would ask some of the younger guys at the winery if they had heard anything about drug gangs in town. If anyone knew, these kids would. He also told her that maybe Greg was just going through the normal teenage growing pains. He did suggest that Susie keep a closer eye on Greg and maybe talk it over with her husband, Mark.

Susie just shook her head and told Jay, "I never see Mark anymore. He's staying in the city more and more for meetings and supposedly sleeping in his office. He doesn't even know that Greg and I exist anymore. He used to be such a good dad, and now he doesn't seem the least bit interested in his son. No wonder Greg is a mess. His parents are a mess."

After dinner, Jay suggested that he and Susie go for a ride around the lake. The weather was beautiful, and a full moon was expected. Jay wanted Susie to himself, but he also thought it would be good for her to get out and relax. They took Jay's car and drove the twenty minutes to the lake and found a quiet place to park under some trees. Jay laid a blanket out on the shore and pulled out a bottle of chilled wine with two glasses. He smiled at Susie and told her, "I hoped you would agree to go for a little ride, so I brought provisions. You never know when you'll need a little medicinal wine for snakebite, or night blindness from a full moon."

Susie laughed and told Jay that he sure had a way with words. She lay back on the blanket and let Jay pour her a glass of the chilled Chardonnay. Jay leaned over Susie and kissed her gently on the neck while telling her how much he missed her. It didn't take long before the two of them were making love under the stars with the sound of the night birds in the background. It was a perfect evening, and it reminded Susie of her youth, of her first love, her first kiss, and her first time. When had her life changed so much? When had she grown up? Why was youth so fleeting? Why can't we feel this wonderful all the time? She was only forty-six; was her love life over? She didn't feel old, and when she was with Jay she felt young and free. She could do anything, be anybody. When had that all changed? When had she and Mark stopped caring about each other?

When Susie and Jay were driving back to Susie's car, Susie was thinking that she had promised herself that she wouldn't have sex with Jay again, that they would just be friends. But she had slipped again, and she didn't feel as guilty as she should have. She didn't know if she loved Jay, but she loved being with him; she loved his gentleness, his considerate lovemaking.

Jay looked over at Susie and said, "Hey, I know you're feeling guilty, but please don't. You and I care deeply for each other, and if we're not in love yet, we are on the way. I care deeply for you, and I'm not going to give you up. Well, if you insist, I will back off. But I don't want to. I will follow your rules and your lead, but I want you to know that I will always be there for you."

Jay dropped Susie off at her car, kissed her, and told her that he'd see her Monday night and to be kind to herself. Susie walked into a silent house. She decided to go to bed early and think about where her relationship with Jay was going. She knew that she and Mark needed to have a real talk about their marriage and their son. Things were not getting any better, just the opposite, and some decisions needed to be made. This unhappiness would spill over onto Greg, if it hadn't already.

Mark was happily wrapped up in Kim's arms in the city. They had enjoyed a leisurely dinner at the wharf, and now they were sharing a bottle of champagne in Kim's bed. Mark had given Kim more clients and more responsibility, and she was very pleased with their relationship. It was a win-win for both of them. Mark got Kim, and she got more contacts, more prestige, and more money. Kim was glad to keep the old fart happy as long as he was useful to her. Once she had established a good clientele, she would dump Mark and move on to someone more her age, and with more zip in bed.

Greg came home after one in the morning, and thank God his mom was in her room with the door closed. Greg needed to lie down; his heart was racing again. He was prepared for it this time—he had bought some Ativan with the money he had gotten from selling his mother's ring. Besides the amphetamines, he now had a supply of the Ativan and enough cash to keep him supplied for the next few weeks. He quickly downed the Ativan with a glass of Coke and waited for his heart to quit racing. He wondered again if the highs and lows were worth it. He had tried to cut back for a few days, but then he felt sick at his stomach, and he had a hard time paying attention in school. He assured himself that he wasn't addicted; he could quit anytime once he really made up his mind.

He liked his new cooler friends and didn't want to go back to hanging out with the geeks that used to be his friends. He was traveling in a new league now, and there was no looking back. His pulse finally settled down, and he was able to fall into a deep sleep.

CHAPTER 37

Joan

Joan and her family had spent a quiet Sunday. Bob had taken off work early from the store, and Brad had ridden his new bike up from Napa to have dinner with his parents and his sister. Joan had made a pot roast and apple pie. She was thrilled to have her whole family together at the table again.

Bob questioned Brad about his job and his girlfriend and asked when they were going to see more of Brad's girlfriend. And what did she think of Brad's motorcycle? Brad told his parents that his girlfriend didn't like the motorcycle either, and she refused to ride on it. Smart girl, his mother thought.

The subject changed to barb's daughter, Lacey. Had Sandy had any luck in finding out what was troubling Lacey? "No, Mom," Sandy said, "but I know whatever is bothering Lacey is serious, and I fully intend on finding out what it is. I have a few ideas, and I think I'm going to snoop around the high school and see if I can pick up any vibes. Some of Lacey's friends must have some suspicions or even know what's going on. I think the school is the place to start, and I'm going over there this week on a day that I have early classes."

Bob warned Sandy not to get in over her head. He told her that he didn't want to have to bail her out of jail. He knew how determined she was when she got into a project; she was like a dog with a bone. He told Sandy she would make a great detective or police officer. Maybe she should go into law enforcement instead of nursing.

Brad teased her that he could just see her wearing a badge and out busting the local teens on Friday nights. He loved his little sister, but also knew how determined she could be. The rest of the evening went well, and Brad headed back to Napa with leftover apple pie.

Monday morning came too soon, with Joan back at work at the hospital. It had been a busy weekend at the hospital with several accidents, and Joan was up to her eyebrows until lunch. When she went to the cafeteria for lunch, she ran into Frank and decided to join him at his table. They exchanged pleasantries and then filled each other in their workload of the morning. Frank had been in surgery much of the weekend. He told her that he thought St. Helena would be a quieter place to practice. "But now I'm beginning to wonder."

Joan assured him that normally St. Helena is a sleepy little town, and it had just been an unusually busy weekend but certainly not the norm. She thought it was often the tourists drinking and driving on the little curvy roads. She had been run off the road more than once by someone driving too fast and not knowing the two-lane highways. Frank asked Joan if she was free after work on Monday night. He wanted to drive into Calistoga and check out a store that he had heard about that sold kitchen supplies, pots and pans, etc. Frank told Joan that he wanted to pick up a Crock-Pot and a few more pans and possibly more dishes. He was tired of eating out, and he thought a Crock-Pot would be ideal for him. He could start a meal in the morning, and it would be done when he got home from the hospital in the evening. He understood that there were also crock-pot recipe books, and he was looking forward to learning to cook. Would Joan go with him since she knew more about Crock-Pots than he did?

Joan agreed that she would be glad to help, but she could only spare two hours since she needed to prepare dinner for Bob and Sandy. "Great," Frank said, "I'll meet you in the parking lot at four. I really appreciate all the time you have spent on me. You are the only real friend that I have made in this town. I don't know what I would have done without you."

Joan called Bob at the store and then Sandy and explained that she might be a little late getting home to fix dinner. Bob told her not to worry about it, that he would be working late on inventory and would grab something at the diner down the street from the store. When Joan talked to Sandy, she told her mom the same thing. She was meeting her study group at the library, and then they were going out for pizza. *Well, okay then,* Joan thought, *I'm not going to worry about rushing home.*

When Joan met Frank in the parking lot at four, she told Frank that she was in no hurry to get home since her family all had made dinner plans, so she was at his full disposal. Frank drove his car, and they reached downtown Calistoga in twenty minutes. The kitchen store was right on the main street between a restaurant and a dress shop.

Frank and Joan looked at several smaller Crock-Pots and picked one that would most suit Frank's needs. They also picked out a saucepan, frying pan, two cookbooks, and some new plates and soup bowls. When Frank was paying for his purchases, he told Joan that cooking was an expensive project, but he was looking forward to getting in the kitchen and trying out his new gear.

Once they had loaded the car with the purchases, Frank looked in the window of the restaurant and told Joan that since she had no one to cook dinner for tonight, he suggested that they grab a quick dinner in the restaurant. It was early enough not to be crowded, and the menu on the window looked very appetizing. Joan agreed as she had eaten there before, and she told Frank that the food served there was excellent.

Once they were seated, Frank ordered two glasses of Pinot for them and then looked at the menu and specials. Joan decided on the chicken Caesar salad, and Frank chose the Philly cheesesteak sandwich with fries. Frank looked around and told Joan that the little restaurant was charming, and the sign in the window advertised live music on the weekends. Maybe he should come up for dinner some weekend night and enjoy the music. He told her that he and his deceased wife had loved to dance, and they tried to get out every few months for a night out with dancing. He told her he may not be a good dancer, but he was an enthusiastic dancer.

Joan said she couldn't remember the last time she and Bob had gone dancing. She had always loved to dance and really missed it, but

Bob had never really enjoyed it and had done it only to please Joan. Frank looked closely at Joan and said, "I don't mean to be intrusive, and you don't have to answer me if you don't want to. But is everything okay between you and Bob? Whenever you and I talk, Bob is always working late or seems preoccupied with the store. I guess what I'm asking is if you're happy."

Joan laid her hand on Frank's hand and answered him, "No, you're not being nosy or intrusive. And I appreciate that you care enough to ask. I'm not sure I'm happy, but after this many years of marriage, I guess this is what happens. Bob is a good provider and a good dad. If things aren't exciting between us anymore, well, maybe that's just the way it's supposed to be. We get settled in our day-to-day lives and families, and maybe we just forget how to be lovers or even friends, but more like companions. Not very romantic sounding. I have asked Bob several times to go away with me for a long weekend, but he's always too busy. And frankly, I'm not sure he cares enough or even wants to spend that much time with me. And maybe I'm afraid to know the truth, so I haven't pushed. It's up to Bob now. I've asked, and I'm not going to ask again."

Frank told Joan how sorry he was and thought Bob was a fool for not taking better care of this wonderful woman, who in his mind should be cherished. He had learned early how precious love and life can be when he lost his wife. He didn't speak his thoughts out loud, but he told Joan that hopefully Bob would wake up before he lost Joan's love.

Joan said she wondered if it was already too late. She wasn't sure what her feelings were for Bob anymore. She felt like she was just going through the motions of being a wife, housekeeper, and mother, and the children were grown. The only place she felt needed was at the hospital where her loving care made a difference to her patients.

Frank totally understood—without medicine, he didn't know how he would survive. He told Joan how lucky he felt that they had so much in common in their love of medicine. They finished their dinner in the relaxed atmosphere, with the conversation focused more on the hospital and fellow staff. The hospital was like a small town with the usual drama and gossip of who was sleeping with whom, and which staff was soon to get the ax for being a slacker.

Frank drove Joan back to her car at the hospital and gave her a hug and then surprised both of them when he reached over and gave Joan a sweet, soft kiss on the lips. Frank immediately apologized and told Joan than he hoped she didn't mind, and he was surprised at himself for his lack of decorum. But he was not sorry for the kiss, and it had been amazing and only too brief. He said that he was starting to have some strong feelings for Joan, and if she didn't return them, he would understand. He also told Joan that no matter what happened, he would always be there for her.

Joan was startled that she had enjoyed this little kiss so much. She knew it was wrong, but she couldn't be mad at Frank; he was so kind and attentive, the opposite of her husband. She knew how lonely he was after losing his wife, and she was glad to be his friend. She told Frank that she wasn't mad and that she had enjoyed the sweet kiss, but she thought that they should keep their relationship strictly on a friendship basis. But yes, she cared for him too.

Frank stood in the parking lot as he watched Joan drive away. He had the feeling that the both of them were heading into deep water, possibly getting in over their heads. But he didn't know how to pull back now or even if he wanted to. He had become very fond of this lovely, caring nurse. Who knew where this friendship would lead, if anywhere at all? He then drove home to his dark, lonely house.

When Joan walked into the house, Bob was already home. He looked up from his newspaper and asked if Joan and Frank had a good time. "Did you help Frank find the pots and pans he was look-ing for? I'm sure you have some recipes you can share with him. Poor guy living alone and cooking his own meals, I'm sure he appreciates all your help. You're a good woman and friend to help a newcomer like that." Then Bob turned back to his newspaper.

Joan asked Bob if he minded her helping Frank out or her spending time with him. Bob said, "No, why would I? I trust you, and you're not that kind of woman. You're a mom, a homemaker, not a trampy cheating woman." He laughed. "I can't even visualize you as a femme fatale. What a crazy thought."

As Joan headed up to bed, she thought, *Well, what a compliment. Bob can't even think of me as a woman. I'm just a housewife. Obviously, I don't have the sex appeal to attract another man. I don't want Bob to be jealous. Well, maybe a little. Then I would know he cares, but it's obvious he doesn't.*

Barb

On Wednesday night, Barb went to Dr. Andrews's office for their first appointment. Barb was noticeably nervous as Dr. Andrews invited Barb into her office and offered her a chair. Dr. Andrews told Barb, "Please don't be nervous." They would discuss only as much as Barb wanted to share. If a subject made barb uncomfortable, then they wouldn't discuss it. Although at some point, the harder issues needed to come to the surface, but only when Barb felt she could trust Dr. Andrews. Now Dr. Andrews asked Barb what had brought her here, what would she like to talk about?

Barb felt sobs coming up in her throat, and the tears were welling up in her eyes. Dr. Andrews handed Barb a tissue and told her to take her time. Just let her feelings out; it was obvious to her that Barb was deeply troubled.

Barb took a deep breath and told her that she was a teacher and a mother of three daughters, and she was married to what appeared to be a drunk and alcoholic, and her oldest daughter was keeping secrets that were obviously making her miserable. But she wouldn't share these secrets with her mother or even her friends. Barb said, "I don't know how to help Lacey, my sixteen-year-old daughter. And I can't get Jack to quit drinking, and he just keeps getting worse. What can I do? I feel so helpless."

"Well," Dr. Andrews said, "you're carrying around a pretty big load by yourself. No wonder you're worn out. First off, you can't help others if you don't help yourself first. You have to take care of your own needs and your health, so that you can then help your family. You can't make your husband quit drinking, only he can do that. You and your family can seek help with AA and groups that work with the family of alcoholics. And maybe you can convince your husband to see me or another professional. But he has to want help. As for your daughter, I would like her to come to the office to meet with me, with or without you. She may also be carrying a big load that she doesn't know how to deal with. In the meantime, show her support. Let her know you love her and that you will be available to listen to her. That there would be no repercussions or anger for anything that she might choose to tell you. She needs to know that there is a nonjudgmental person in her corner. She needs to feel safe to tell you anything.

"The teenage years are hard enough without extra pressure being added on. Do you think Lacey is involved in drugs or a sexual relationship that is damaging? How is she doing in school? Her grades? Is she losing weight or dressing differently? How are her friends responding to her? There can be many possibilities for her change in behavior. We won't know until we talk to her and if she's willing to talk with you or me."

Joan told Dr. Andrews that her grades seemed to be fine. She was eating less, dressing in baggier clothes, and spending more and more time alone in her room and not hanging out with her friends like she used to. Joan knew that something serious was going on with Lacey, but Lacey just wouldn't talk about it. Joan was up against a brick wall and didn't know how to break down Lacey's wall.

Dr. Andrews told Barb that she should watch Lacey for signs of a possible eating disorder but also let Lacey know that Barb was willing to hear anything that Lacey had to tell her. Dr. Andrews would like to see Lacey in her office in the next few weeks, if Lacey would agree. She would also like to see Barb back in the office the next week. She also told Barb to be kind to herself and hang on. And she should feel free to call Dr. Andrews at any time if things seemed to change for the worse. As far as Barb's husband was concerned, he would have to make his own decisions about his drinking. At some point, Barb may reach a point where she was not willing to put up with Bob's behavior. She assured Barb that she would know when that time came.

Barb went home feeling lighter. She had shared her fears with someone, and she didn't feel so alone. Dr. Andrews had been kind and not shocked by anything Barb had told her. Barb would thank Joan for the referral. When Barb got home, she started dinner and checked on the girls. Rachel and Brenda were doing their homework in front of the TV, and Lacey was in her room. Jack was not home from work yet, or maybe he had stopped off for a beer with one of his buddies.

Barb told the younger girls that she would start dinner in a minute and then went upstairs to talk to Lacey. She knocked on Lacey's door and asked if she could come in and talk to her for a minute. Lacey gave the okay, and Barb went in and sat down on Lacey's bed next to Lacey.

Barb told Lacey that she had gone to see a therapist, a psychologist to help her with her problems and to have someone to talk to. She also told Lacey that she felt better after talking to Dr. Andrews, that Dr. Andrews had listened and given her a few suggestions. Barb also suggested that Lacey join her at one of these sessions, either with or without her mother.

Lacey looked at her mother and said, "Mom what kind of problems do you have? You're an adult, a teacher. No one can intimidate you. You have a nice house, friends. What possible problems can you have?"

"Really, Lacey, what problems do I have? Have you looked at your father lately? He's normally intoxicated when he's at home or even when he's not at home. I haven't wanted to make an issue of it with you kids, but your dad is an alcoholic, and I've been an enabler by not speaking up more. I either have to learn to live with it, or take you girls and move out, or kick your dad out. I am also worried sick about you and whatever problem that you have and won't share with us. It's obvious that something is terribly wrong and worrying you, and I want you to know that you can tell me anything. Nothing you tell me will shock or upset me. I will always be there for you. I love you, and your problems are my problems."

Lacey squeezed her mom's hand and said, "I love you too, but I don't think any therapist can help me and my problems. I have to deal with them myself, and I'm working on it. I'm glad you're seeing someone to help you with dad's problems. The girls and I have known for years that dad has a drinking problem, and I don't know how you have put up with it all of these years. You are either a saint or a glutton for punishment. I would have kicked him out a long time ago. You deserve better than that, Mom, and I am so sorry for you. I don't have any respect for dad anymore. I may love him, but I don't like him."

"Oh sweetie," Barb said, "I didn't realize that you and the girls were so aware of dad's drinking. I tried to keep you girls out of our problems. I didn't want you to think badly of him. I married him, and it was my problem to deal with, not yours. I am so sorry. Please think about going with me to Dr. Andrews next week. I think she could really help you. Just think about it. I won't push, I promise."

Lacey said she would think about it, and she'd come down when dinner was ready. Lacey felt really sorry for her mom and the pain that she and her dad were causing her, but hopefully Lacey's problem would go away soon, for sure once the school year ended. Lacey pulled her razor blade out from underneath her mattress, promising herself that this would be the last time she used it.

CHAPTER 39

Maggie

Thursday night after bocce, the four women met up for their after-bocce glass of wine. They were in a good mood after winning two out of three games. They settled down at a table, and Susie asked for four glasses, since she had brought a bottle of Zinfandel from her winery. The ladies ordered a platter of nachos to go with the Zin. Susie told the others that they'd better like this wine since she had made it herself. It had a nice nose, and it was not too peppery.

"Great," Maggie said. "Note the fancy words—*nose* and *peppery*—it sounds like we're talking about a skunk and not a bottle of wine. Such talk, Susie. Way to make it sound tasty." Once the ladies had taken a sip, they did have to admit that it was a very nice wine.

Joan agreed and told them that whenever she found a bottle of wine she really liked, that meant that she couldn't afford it. She admitted that she bought most of her wine at Trader Joe's, Costco, or BevMo! Once the nachos were delivered, the ladies dug in and discussed the mistakes they had made to lose the last game. The team hadn't been that tough but had just outplayed the ladies.

"Next week," Barb said, "we'll win all three games. This team got us at a weak moment. But if we all lift weights this week, we can take next week's team." Barb then turned to Joan and told her, "I just wanted to thank you for the referral to Dr. Andrews." She had thought Dr. Andrews kind and helpful, and she was urging Lacey to go with her the following week.

Joan told Barb that she was so glad that she had liked Dr. Andrews and that she has a great reputation at the hospital. Barb gave the other women a brief outline of her conversation with Dr. Andrews, and that just talking with her once had made her feel more empowered.

Maggie said, "Maybe I should suggest a visit to Jeff since he's been on the mopey side lately. Although he did have a date with a new girl last week. He seemed excited when he came home and more cheerful than I've seen him for a while. So whoever this girl is, I hope it lasts. It's hard to see your child hurting, and you can't or he won't let you help him."

"I know how you feel," Barb said. "Lacey won't let me in on her problems either. She's breaking my heart. I just hope she'll agree to meet with Dr. Andrews sometime soon. Now I think we should change the subject to something more exciting like Susie's love life or Joan's friendship with Dr. Frank. Maybe I need some handsome young stud or a famous doctor in my life. I need to kick up my heels a little or let down my hair. Or better yet, let some handsome guy rub my feet and run his fingers through my hair." The other women laughed, and the subject was changed.

After an hour, the women departed for home, promising to get in a longer practice on Tuesday night and to keep in touch over the weekend.

When Maggie got home, Tom was watching a movie and told her that Jeff had called, and he was out with a friend but had promised to be home by ten. What Tom didn't tell Maggie was that he had just gotten home himself. He and Sharon had gone out for a glass of wine once they closed the office. Sharon had suggested to Tom that she had a few ideas to improve things at the office and thought it would be better to discuss her ideas outside of the office in a more relaxed atmosphere.

Tom had to admit that Sharon did have some good suggestions, although he wasn't sure he was ready to agree to some of these improvements. Sharon had suggested massaging chairs and small TVs in every patient room, and a bookcase full of new novels and magazines in the waiting room. The office already offered music for their patients and magazines, but heated massage chairs and TVs were a little over the top and a very expensive project and one that he wasn't sure that he could afford at that point.

Sharon had also made it obvious that she wanted to become a full partner in the practice, and sooner than the five years that Tom had originally suggested when Sharon had signed on with the practice. He had to admire her ambition and tenacity. She would make her points by touching Tom's hands, or rubbing the back of his neck, when describing the need for the massage chairs. She was very attractive as well as persuasive; it was hard for Tom not to succumb to her charms. He ended up telling Sharon that he would think about her suggestions and discuss them with his business manager and accountant. She agreed and told him that they could get together in another week or two for another drink and private chat. When they were leaving the bar, Sharon leaned over and gave Tom a big hug, leaving a trail of her amazing perfume in her wake.

Jeff had driven to Calistoga to meet with Joey, Sarah's friend. He had scheduled the meeting for Tuesday night, but he had to change to Thursday night when he had to cram for a chemistry test scheduled for Wednesday morning. Jeff was not as nervous as he had been when he approached the house, although he was a bit apprehensive about meeting with Joey.

Sarah opened the door and invited Jeff in and introduced him to Joey, an attractive young man in his midtwenties. Joey led Jeff upstairs and suggested that they just chat for a few minutes and get acquainted. Joey told Jeff that Sarah had basically explained Jeff's query and that Joey would Be glad to answer any questions or help if he could. He also explained his fee schedule to Jeff, and told him that it was totally up to Jeff if he wanted to go further than just talking. It was totally up to Jeff as to how far this went.

Jeff basically told Joey that he had to know if he was gay or not, if something was wrong with him. He was so confused and didn't want to get involved with a fellow schoolmate. And the last thing he wanted to do was be laughed at or, worse, humiliated. Joey suggested that they spend an hour together and see where things led. Joey would be gentle and professional, and then hopefully Jeff would have his answer one way or the other. Joey explained that he knew he was gay by the time he was fourteen, but he didn't have the courage to come out until he was twenty. His parents had not been accepting and had thrown him out of the house. Joey was working a few hours doing this and working part-time as a checker in a grocery store while attending some college classes.

After an hour of Joey's gentleness, Jeff was pretty sure that this was the life he was destined to lead. Jeff was relieved but also fearful of how to proceed, how to tell his parents and his friends. He knew his older brother, Michael, would understand, and he would tell Michael first. Maybe Michael would come down, and they could tell their parents together. He could hold off telling his friends; there was no need for him to include them in this secret. He needed to know from Joey how to go about meeting other single guys like him.

Joey sat down with Jeff and told him that he knew he would have lots of questions. The first and most important thing to remember was be safe, use protection, be selective in your partners, and get tested just as you would in a heterosexual relationship. He said that nowadays most people were pretty broad-minded and will understand and not think less of him and be supportive of his decision. But there are also those people out there that will judge him, be unkind and call him names, and bully him. These were small-minded people, but their words could still be painful. As far as finding someone to care about to get involved with, he shouldn't rush it. It would happen when the time was right, but he should be discerning and cautious. There were predators out there and especially with the Internet, so he warned Jeff to be cautious and wise. Joey gave Jeff his phone number and told him that if he ever had a question, to please give him a call.

Joey also told Jeff that he had been in a committed relationship for the last two years, and he hoped that Jeff would find that kind of relationship someday. Joey gave Jeff a hug, and said, "Be safe out there, my friend, and be smart. And always trust your gut."

Jeff drove home with so many thoughts going through his head. Would his parents still love and accept him? Mom maybe, Dad always talked about being so macho; hopefully he loved Jeff enough to understand. Jeff vowed to call Michael first thing in the morning and ask him to come home for a weekend to be back up for when Jeff told his parents.

Jeff walked into the house a few minutes before ten. His mom was reading a book, and his dad had gone to bed. Maggie asked Jeff if he had fun, and was he with his new friend Sarah? He told his mom that he had been with Sarah, and she had introduced him to another new friend, Joey. Maggie told Jeff that she was so glad he was making new friends and to please feel free to have them over for dinner some evening. Jeff just laughed to himself as he went upstairs to bed. *Not going to happen, Mom., I don't think you want two prostitutes in your house for dinner. They are both very nice but still not your normal dinner guests.*

CHAPTER 40

Susie

Friday night, Susie had agreed to meet Jay again and go for a drive up to the lake. Mark had told Susie that he was staying over in the city, and Greg would be out with friends; so she had offered to pack a picnic dinner of cold chicken salad, bread, and chocolates and Jay would bring the wine. Susie made a quick trip to the deli for the dinner, and she would meet Jay at the local elementary school, so they could drive up in Jay's car. Mark hadn't even bothered to explain to her why he was staying over, and she didn't care enough to ask anymore. They were both going their own ways and living their own lives. Sometimes Susie wondered what had happened to the two of them and why had they grown so far apart. But most of the time Susie didn't care.

Jay and Susie reached the lake by seven and laid out their picnic on a blanket on a secluded shore of the lake. They enjoyed the first glass of wine as they caught up on each other's news. Susie told Jay about the ladies' bocce game, and Jay filled Susie in on the new wine that he was working on. He was having a hard time getting the mix right, and maybe Susie had some suggestions. She offered to swing by his winery on Monday and taste a sample and make some helpful hints. She thought Jay was a talented winemaker, and she wasn't sure that she could improve on his efforts. Sometimes you just have to keep trying different mixes until you get the wanted results.

Once they had eaten, they lay back, looking at the stars and just enjoying the evening. They made love again, and by now Susie didn't even try to delude herself that they shouldn't or that it was wrong. She didn't care anymore, and she loved being with Jay. He was so different from Mark—so gentle, so caring, always putting her needs before his. Mark had been a selfish lover, at least in the last few years. Actually, Mark hadn't touched Susie in over eight months. She was pretty sure he wasn't just working all those nights in San Francisco, but again she just didn't care. What does that say when you don't care if your husband is cheating on you? But then she was cheating on him, so they were even.

While they just lay there enjoying the night, Jay leaned over and said to Susie, "Babe, I don't want to pressure you. But where do see our relationship going? I'd like to think that someday we can have a more permanent relationship. If not marriage, at least a commitment. I don't need children necessarily, and I don't imagine you want any more children. And I'm okay with that. I don't need to be a father. I can share your son. We can do guy things—baseball games, bowling—whatever Greg likes. I know I'm younger than you, but I'm not a kid, and I want to settle down one of these days. We could adopt a dog or cat, even a bunny, your choice. What do you think?"

Susie said, "Wow, Jay, that's a lot to think about. I think I love you, and yes, I would love to spend more time with you, maybe permanently. But I think we need more time to get to know each other. You haven't even met Greg, and I don't begin to know what to do about Mark. My husband and I don't even talk anymore. I want you to meet Greg. I just have to figure out the best way to do it. Do I introduce you as my lover? A friend from work? Greg seems to be such a mess right now. I can't even reach him. He has shut me out. I'm going to suggest he meet with a therapist that Joan knows, a Dr. Andrews. Maybe she can reach Greg. I worry that he's hanging out with a bad crowd. I haven't caught him at anything yet, but I still feel like the kid is up to something. Maybe I should have him followed or follow him myself. I'll drive a strange rented car and be like Nancy Drew on the hunt. What do you think? Should I wear a wig and sunglasses?"

Jay laughed. "That sounds perfect. And you are my favorite sleuth. But seriously, if you think something is really going on with

Greg, you need to get to the bottom of it before he gets into some real trouble. Fifteen-year-old boys are full of hormones and crazy ideas. He needs a watchful parent, preferably a dad, but kids need supervision. If you ever need my help, just let me know. I was a teenage boy once too."

Greg had gone out with his new gang buddies on Friday night, and as usual their first item on the agenda was to get high. The leader, Shane, suggested that they needed more beer and maybe some whiskey or Tequila to round out the evening. Shane suggested a small liquor store in Napa that he knew, which was usually staffed by just one elderly employee.

They drove to Napa in two cars, and once outside the liquor store, Shane suggested that one of the other guys distract the employee and buy some beer while Greg ran in and grabbed one or two bottles of whiskey, tequila, or whatever he could grab. Greg said, "Hey, wait. Shane, are you asking me to steal liquor? I've never stole anything before except from my Mom, and I don't want to go to jail."

Shane told Greg to consider it an initiation into the club, and if he really wanted to be a part of the gang, he needed to man up. The old guy was alone, and it should be a piece of cake. He told Greg that if he was going to be a pussy, he didn't belong with this group, and he could go back to the nerds that he used to hang with.

Greg finally agreed and casually walked into the store while one of the other guys grabbed two six packs of beer and started chatting up the old man. Greg walked to the back wall of the store and grabbled two bottles of whiskey and hid them under his jacket and coolly strolled out of the store. Shane and the others were waiting for Greg, and Shane said, "Told you, piece of cake. Now next time you won't be so nervous."

The clerk saw Greg put some bottles under his coat but waited until both young men were out of the store before he went over to check the section and noticed the missing bottles. The clerk then called the police to report the theft. He hadn't wanted to confront the kids since he was alone, and they looked high and could be potentially dangerous. He made sure he went to the window and got a good look at the car that they were driving.

The guys took their beer and whiskey to a park downtown and passed around the liquor and chips. Greg was feeling pretty sure of himself by this time. He had proved himself to the guys. The other guys carried fake IDs, and Greg would ask Shane if they could get him a fake ID too. Shane was right, these guys were much cooler than his other buddies. Jeff would never think of getting high or stealing booze, but then Jeff was a pussy.

While they were at the park, Greg started feeling sick. His heart was racing again, and he was nauseated. And his vision was getting blurry. *What the hell? What is this about?* he thought. *I have never felt like this before.* And even then, he was breaking out into a sweat. Greg said to Shane, "Hey, I'm not feeling real well. Must be the flu or something, Can one of you drop me off at home?"

"Yeah," Shane agreed. He would have one of the guys take Greg home, and then they could continue to party. Shane asked Greg, had he taken any unusual or new pills or drugs other than what he normally took? He thought he saw Greg buying more stuff than usual. Greg said, "Well, yeah, I'm just trying something new. And it was cheaper. And I get more pills for my buck, so why not?"

Shane told Greg not to be a fool; you never knew what was in the stuff. It could be laced with cocaine and get him high but also kill him. Greg was sure he was fine, probably just the flu, but he did want to go home. He just needed to take some Ativan to calm him down. No biggie.

Shane had Sammie drive Greg home, and then Sammie could meet up with the guys later to continue to party. Maybe they'd pick up some girls and really have a party. The night was still young.

The police arrived at the liquor store, and the clerk gave the description of the car and the two young men who had come into the store. He had seen the one boy that bought the beer before, but the kid that had taken the whiskey was new to him. He thought the boy looked really young, though. The police officer told the clerk that they would keep an eye out for the car, but it was a theft with no weapons, so it wasn't as pressing as other crimes. The officer did tell the clerk that they had noticed that drug usage was up in the local schools, and they would love to catch the bastard that was supplying the kids.

Greg got home and went straight for his stash of Ativan stored under his mattress. He took the pill. But fifteen minutes later, he was still feeling sick and sweating profusely, when a sharp pain hit him in his chest. He doubled over and could barely stand with the pain. His vision was getting blurry, and he was vomiting on himself. He had to get help, find his mom. He made it down the stairs until he collapsed on the hall floor, unconscious, and lying in his own vomit.

Susie walked into the house at eleven thirty and nearly tripped over Greg lying on the hallway floor by the stairs. "Oh my god, Greg, are you all right?" Was he drunk? Had he fallen? He smelled like vomit. Maybe he was drunk; that was bad but not serious. She shook him, trying to wake him up, but there was no response.

She then tried to check his breathing, but it was very shallow, and his color was gray. She needed to get help; maybe he had fallen and hit his head. She ran to the phone and called 911 and then not knowing what else to do, she called Joan, who lived just down the street, and as a nurse she would know what to do.

When Joan answered, Susie sobbingly told Joan that Greg was sick, unconscious, and lying on the floor. Joan told her to calm down, call 911, and she was on her way. "Just hang on," she told her, "hang on." Joan was still dressed and ran all the way up the street and got there just as the paramedics pulled up. She knew both of the medics and said a quick hi as they rushed into Susie's house. Susie was standing on the front porch, screaming to hurry.

Joan and the paramedics quickly appraised Greg's color and respiration, and they knew he was in trouble. They could smell alcohol on his breath, but his vitals indicated something more serious. They quickly took the necessary measures and then told Susie that they needed to transport him to the local hospital. Susie could ride with them or follow in her car. "No," Susie sobbed, "I'll ride with you. Joan, will you come with me?"

Joan gave Susie a hug and told her that she would get her car and follow them to the hospital. She grabbed Susie's purse that she had dropped on the floor and told her to go with Greg, and she'd be right there. Joan ran home, told Bob what had happened, and told him she was going to the hospital with Susie. Bob told her of course she should go and please keep him posted. Joan grabbed her purse and her keys and headed for the hospital. She prayed all the way to the hospital. Greg hadn't looked good. Something was definitely not right. Was Greg involved in drugs? She had seen that look before in other patients, and she was very afraid for Greg and Susie.

Joan found Susie sitting in the emergency room waiting room, totally hysterical and sobbing. Susie told Joan that they had given Greg oxygen in the ambulance and then had gone some chest compressions, and then they started an IV. The medic wouldn't tell her what was happening. "Why won't they tell me what's wrong? What's happening? He's my baby, my only child. He can't die. Tell me he won't die. Tell me, Joan. And tell me he's going to be all right."

Joan hugged Susie and tried to reassure her that Greg would be okay. She explained that the doctors needed to run some blood tests and possibly an EKG and scans to find out what was wrong with Greg. Joan said to Susie, "I hate to ask you this, but has Greg been doing any kind of drugs? Have you noticed anything different about him lately?"

"Well," Susie said between sobs, "he's been hanging out with a different group of guys lately. He's been closed off from me, and Mark is never around. Greg has been more secretive and staying out later. But I haven't noticed any signs of drug use. Oh my god, what's going to happen to him?"

Joan suggested that Susie call Mark. He had a right to know that his son was in the hospital. Joan told Susie to give her Mark's number, and she would call him with the news. But when Joan called Mark's cell phone, it went right to voice mail. Then she tried Mark's office, where she knew he often slept when staying in the city, but there was no answer. Joan left a message to call her that Greg was ill, and please return to St. Helena and to the hospital.

Joan then went back and sat with Susie for the next two hours until one of the doctors came out to talk to Susie. He asked Susie the same question as Joan—had Greg been taking any kind of drugs or amphetamines? "No," Joan said, "no, not that I'm aware of. It's hard to get a vitamin down him or aspirin, let alone drugs. What's wrong with Greg? Do you know what's wrong with him? Will he be okay? Please tell me he's going to be okay."

The emergency room doctor told Susie and Joan that he would like to call in Dr. Harris, a cardiologist, that Greg was showing signs of heart arrhythmia, and he had not regained consciousness. He was concerned about Greg's heart, and he would like him to be examined by a specialist. The doctor assured Susie that Dr. Harris was one of the best in the valley. Joan reached over and touched Susie's hand and told her that she knew Dr. Frank Harris well, and he was wonderful, that she could totally trust him.

Susie asked Joan, "Is this the Doctor Frank that you've been helping with his new home and spending time with?"

"Yes," Joan told her, "and he's a great doctor as well as a very kind person. Everyone here at the hospital trusts and respects him. If it were my child, I would want Frank on my side. He's the best. He'll know what to do."

Jay called Susie at midnight just to say good night as he sometimes did, and Susie told Jay that she was at the hospital, and her son Greg was seriously ill, although the doctors didn't know what was wrong yet. Through tears, she said to Jay, "You and I were making love while my son was lying in his own vomit, possibly dying. How can I live with myself? How can I ever face my son again? I let him down. I have let everyone down. What kind of a mother am I?"

Jay told Susie that she couldn't think like that. She was a good mother. She was home every night, cooked his meals, helped with his homework, and loved him unconditionally. "You need to wait to find out what's wrong with him. Maybe it's not serious. Maybe it's some kind of flu, but you can't blame yourself." He wanted to know how Greg's Father was taking it. Was he being helpful, or was he blaming Susie too?

"No," Susie told him, "Mark doesn't even know that Greg is sick. He's not answering his phone. Joan's been calling him, but no, he doesn't know. He hasn't been there for Greg in months."

Jay said, "I'm coming to the hospital. You shouldn't be alone now. I want to be with you."

Susie told him not now. Joan was with her, and hopefully Mark would show up at some point. She assured Jay that she would let him know as soon as she knew more. Once they heard more from Dr. Harris, then hopefully they would all know more.

Dr. Harris arrived at the hospital, gave Joan a hug, and was introduced to Susie. He promised Susie that he would do his very best for Greg and would let her know more once he examined him. He told Susie to keep the faith and suggested that Joan take Susie to the cafeteria for a cup of coffee or tea.

Good idea, Joan thought, and grabbed Susie's arm and dragged her down the hall to the cafeteria. Susie didn't want to leave, but Joan assured her that Frank needed some time to spend with Greg and examine him. Joan said she could use a strong cup of coffee, since her friend had dragged her out of bed. However, Joan's humor was lost on Susie, and Joan apologized and just sat her down in a chair and put a cup of coffee in front of Susie.

Dr. Harris spent two hours with Greg before he came back to talk to Susie and Joan. Greg had gone into cardiac arrest once, and it had been touch and go for a few minutes. Greg was stabilized now or for the time being, but he was definitely not out of the woods. He had not regained consciousness, and his vitals were still unstable.

Frank went back into the waiting room to talk to Susie and Joan. Susie looked like she was going to fall apart any minute. Her hands were shaking, her eyes were teary, and she was very pale. Frank sat down in a chair across from Susie and told her what he was sure she wouldn't want to hear. He started out quietly. "Susie, may I call you Susie? I think your son has suffered a heart attack, possibly from drug use or maybe cocaine. I saw quite a bit of this when I worked in the Chicago hospital. It's unusual for someone as young as Greg to have a heart attack, but if he was using drugs, it puts a strong load on the heart. Amphetamines, cocaine, and other illegal substances can trigger heart arrhythmia and result in a heart attack and even death. I've ordered some blood work and toxicology work to see what substances or drugs we may find in Greg's blood, which will tell us more. In the meantime, we need to keep a very close eye on him. I would feel better if he would wake up, but we'll just have to see. The next twenty-four hours will be crucial. I'm so sorry I can't give you better news. I will check in with you in a few hours."

Frank pulled Joan aside and told her to keep an eye on her friend. "I am honestly concerned for this kid. And just between you and me, I do think drugs are behind this." He then gave Joan a quick hug and went back to check on Greg.

At seven in the morning, Jay called Susie again and asked if there had been any change, and how was Greg doing? Susie told Jay what Dr. Harris had said, that Greg might have suffered a heart attack from doing drugs. She just couldn't believe that her son would be so stupid to get involved with drugs, but she didn't feel like she knew her son at all anymore. Until Greg woke up—if he woke up—they would never know what had caused this. At this point, Susie was just praying for Greg to wake up.

Jay asked again if he could come to the hospital to be with Susie, but again she said no, she would keep in touch and let him know if anything changed. Jay told her to hang on and then he said, "Look, Susie, if I can't be there to help you, then I'm going to find out who in the hell is giving drugs to high school kids. I'm been asking around and heard and got a few hints but nothing serious. Well, now I have the whole weekend and a real incentive to find the SOB that is giving these kids drugs. And then I'll kill the SOB. I'll be in touch. And remember, I love you."

Susie hung up and thought that Jay who had never even met Greg seemed to care more than his own dad, who she still couldn't get in touch with. She and Joan had tried calling Mark all night, but still no answer. At this point, Susie didn't care if she never heard from him again. What was more important to Mark than his son?

Jay got dressed in some old ripped jeans and set off to find himself a drug dealer. Jay thought if he looked down and out enough, he might convince others that he was a user, and they would give him some names. He would start at the local pool hall, hit a few bars, and see if anyone was willing to talk. He went to the ATM to get some extra cash. Maybe that would help him be more persuasive.

Saturday afternoon at two, Mark finally listened to his voice mails. He and Kim had gone out for a leisurely brunch and then did a little window-shopping. He had planned to drive back to St. Helena around five, after one more quick romp with Kim. She was intoxicating, and it was becoming more and more difficult to leave her. Once he heard the frantic voice mails from Joan and Susie, he was startled, upset, sick to his stomach, and—yes—guilty. He told Kim that his son was ill, and he had to leave immediately. He called Susie and told her that his phone had died, and he had just gotten the message. And how was Greg?

Susie told Mark that frankly she didn't care why Mark hadn't called, but that she had her suspicions, but none of that mattered now. All that mattered was their son. She told Mark that Greg was still unconscious or was in a coma, and the doctors thought he had suffered a heart attack from possibly using drugs. She said, "Mark, if you want to be here, fine. If not, fine, I really could care less. All I care about is our son, and I just pray that he survives. We can deal with the drug issues later, if there is a later." She hung up crying.

He drove back to St. Helena in just under ninety minutes. He went straight to the hospital and found Susie and Joan sitting in the waiting room. When he walked in and sat down, Joan told them that she would give them some privacy. She needed to go home, take a shower, and spend an hour or so with her family. She told Susie she would be back by six and would bring soup and sandwiches. She gave Susie a hug and asked her to call if there was any change.

Mark sat down next to Susie and asked her to tell him everything, how this had happened, when had it happened. Was she with him? Susie filled him in on the details, and then she told Mark that she was going up to the chapel to pray. When she left the room, Mark was sobbing into his hands.

Joan went home to find Sandy sitting in the kitchen doing homework, and Bob was at the store. Joan told Sandy the whole story about Greg and the possibility that Greg had been doing drugs. Sandy said to Joan, "Mom, do you think that's what is bothering Lacey? Could she be into drugs? She and Greg go to the same school, have some of the same friends. Could this be why Lacey is acting so weird?"

Joan told Sandy that she just didn't know, and she certainly hoped not. Joan said her heart was just breaking for Susie, and all she could do was be there for her, be supportive, and bring dinner. Sandy said, "Well, I can do more, and I will. I'm going to the high school on Monday after class and do some snooping. I'm going to talk to some of Lacey's friends and teachers. I'm going to find out what the hell is wrong and why Lacey has withdrawn from everyone. Something is just not right."

Joan went upstairs to shower and change, call Bob at the store to tell him what was happening, and then she would go to the deli to pick up soup and sandwiches to take to Susie and Mark. Bob suggested that she lay down for an hour and grab a nap before she headed back to the hospital. Joan had to admit she was exhausted; she had been up all night. She agreed to lie down for an hour or two and then go back to the hospital.

Jay had spent his day talking to guys in the local bars and pool halls. Most of those that he questioned just brushed him off, but a couple of the guys were willing to talk, especially when he offered a little financial incentive. He was hearing the same story about a guy that worked in a local garage that had moved here from Las Vegas. He was considered a tough guy, someone you didn't want to mess with. The story was that this guy had done some time for pushing drugs and assault. He didn't get a name yet, but one of the guys he spoke to offered to find out more and call Jay back. It was a start, and at least he felt like he was helping Susie.

When Joan got back to the hospital with dinner for Susie and Mark, she was told by Susie that Greg had woken up, but he was in and out of consciousness. The Doctor just wanted him to rest. Greg was in the ICU coronary unit. They were waiting to hear more from Dr. Harris. Joan sat down with them and encouraged them both to eat just a little bit. They needed to keep up their strength, and at some point Susie was going to need to get some sleep.

Dr. Harris walked into the waiting room at seven and told Susie and Mark that even though Greg was awake, he was not really aware of his surroundings or what had happened. He had suffered a myocardial infarction, a severe heart attack, and it would be touch and go for the next few days. They were keeping him comfortable and heavily medicated. His parents could sit with him for a few minutes every hour, but not question him or overtire him, just sit with him, hold his hand, and talk softly. Let him know they were there, but no pushing for answers. "We'll know more when Greg can talk or when we get the toxicology reports back. I'm so sorry," he said. "I can't tell you more or give you more hope, but the fact he's still with us is a good sign. I will continue to check in with him all night, and hopefully we'll know more tomorrow or Monday. The nurse will take you in to see Greg now."

Frank then took Joan by the arm and told her he was taking her to the cafeteria for some dinner, and there was no sense arguing with him because she looked exhausted, and he would not accept a no. So that was that. She was quick to agree, and she would love to sit down for a minute and have a cup of tea and maybe a salad.

Frank said he felt so bad for Susie and the poor kid. He was pretty sure that Greg had used drugs, but he was not going to say that to Greg's parents until he knew for sure. He just couldn't understand why a nice kid like Greg would even go down that road. Both Frank and Joan knew that if Greg survived this, he would need to go into rehab and most likely therapy. He told Joan that it was such a waste of young lives. He had seen more than his share of drug deaths, and he was just sick of it. He thought he had left that all behind him in Chicago. But no, here it was again in this little town in the wine country.

Frank told Joan that he was glad to see her, although it should have been under better circumstances. "I feel like that old song 'I've Grown Accustomed to Her Face.'" He told her that he missed talking to her and hated going home to his quiet little house.

Joan laughed and said, "That's it, Frank, you and I are going to the local animal shelter and find you a pet. You could have a dog, cat, hamster, or even a turtle. A pet to talk to at the end of the day, a dog or cat to snuggle with. You know what they say: a dog is man's best friend. Next week we are going pet shopping, I insist."

Frank thought about it and said, "Aye aye, captain, maybe a parrot. But seriously, I think I would like to have a pet. I had a dog when I was growing up, and he was wonderful, my best friend. You're on pet shopping next week, once we pull Greg through this mess."

Joan left the hospital at nine and told Susie that she needed to get some sleep. Joan would come back the next morning, and for Susie to call if there was a change or if she needed anything. When Joan got home, she called Maggie and Barb to tell them the terrible news about Greg. She asked that they not go to the hospital but pray for Greg, and she would call them on Sunday with more updates.

Susie told Mark that she would only go home long enough to take a shower and change, and then if he wanted, he could go home after she came back. But she didn't want Greg to be alone at the hospital.

Susie was fine with curling up on a couch in the lobby to catch a little sleep. Mark agreed that he would stay until Susie got back, and he was glad to stay too. Mark wanted to call Kim and tell her what was going on. Suddenly, Kim didn't seem as important to him. When Mark called Kim, she told him she was out with friends. She was sorry to hear about Greg, but her voice didn't sound sorry, and he could hear male laughter in the background. He began to wonder how Kim spent her time when she wasn't with him.

When Susie got home, she called Jay to tell him about Greg's diagnosis and that Mark had finally made an appearance. Jay told Susie that he had been out all day checking on possible drug pushers in the area. He felt like he was on the right track and was hoping to get some names in the next few days.

He said, "I love you, Susie, hang in there. You're going to make it, and so is Greg. Just hang on and be strong."

"God, I hope so, Jay. I hope so," Susie told Jay as she said good night, as she headed for the shower and then back to the hospital.

Joan

By the time Joan got home, both Bob and Sandy were waiting for her to hear the latest news on Greg. Joan filled them in on Greg's progress and the diagnosis of a heart attack. Both Bob and Sandy were stunned that someone so young could have a heart attack. Bob was dismayed to hear that Mark had been unavailable, and he hadn't realized that Susie and Mark were having problems. Bob said, "You never know what happens in someone else's home, or what goes on in their lives. I always thought they were the power couple, Susie a fancy winemaker and Mark a big-time money-making stockbroker. I guess money doesn't buy happiness."

Sandy told them that she too was worried about Greg, and she had been making some calls that afternoon to mutual friends to see if any of their friends knew or thought that maybe Greg was into drugs. She told her parents that she had been discreet, but she wanted to know if they thought that Greg had been acting differently. Several of the guys had told her that Greg had been hanging out with a new crowd, and they thought the gang leader, Shane, was trouble. He was older than Greg, nineteen or so, had the reputation of being in trouble with the law, was a high school dropout, and basically not a very nice guy. He traveled with a crowd of younger guys that seemed to look up to him with hero worship, although from what she had heard, Greg was the youngest of Shane's followers.

Joan thought all this sounded worse than she had thought. She wasn't sure if she should tell this to Susie or wait until Greg was better. She didn't want to give her untold worry. Bob thought that his parents needed to know. He said, "If it was my son hanging with hoodlums, I'd want to know. Maybe I'll say something to Mark at the appropriate time when Greg is better."

Sandy warned both of her parents to be careful of what they said to either Susie or Mark until they knew more about Greg's friends and activities. She told them she wasn't through snooping around. She had some other contacts she wanted to check with. She was going to go by the high school on Monday to check out Lacey's problem and maybe find out more about Greg.

Bob gave Sandy a hug, and said, "My own Nancy Drew on the case. What would we do without your sleuthing work? If I remember right, you grew up reading Nancy Drew. That's what happened to you. Remember I asked Brad to have dinner with us on Monday night? I want to ask him if he'd like to come into the store with me as my assistant and someday maybe take over the store. I can add 'Son' to the end of the store's name. What do you two think?"

Joan said, "Oh my gosh, you're right. I almost forgot that Brad was coming to dinner. I'll shop tomorrow and pick up a roast or maybe make burgundy beef and a chocolate cake. I love to spoil him since I see him so seldom. I'll spend part of the day at the hospital with Susie, and then I'll come home and cook."

Sunday, Joan did exactly that—she spent the morning with Susie at the hospital, and then she went to the grocery store in the afternoon and made a banana cake with chocolate peanut butter frosting. The Elvis cake, unusual but yummy, and it was one of Brad's favorites.

Greg's condition was still unchanged—no worse, no better. So telling Susie that she would be available if needed, she left the hospital. Both Barb and Maggie had called and offered to come to the hospital but being told that there was nothing they could do, they both told her they would pray for Greg.

Sunday night after dinner, Joan decided to go to bed early and read. Bob was staying downstairs to watch a movie, and Sandy was in her room on her phone with friends. She had been making calls about her suspicions that she intended to follow up on Monday afternoon. She was hearing rumors about a certain male teacher, and she wanted to check it out.

Joan went into the hospital early on Monday morning; she wanted to check on Greg and Susie before she went on her shift. She found Susie sound asleep in a chair in the waiting room, and the night nurse told her that Mark had gone home around two in the morning to catch some sleep. Both parents were taking turns going home to shower or eat. The nurse also told Joan that Mark and Susie didn't spend much time talking to each other. Maybe it was just their way of coping with this tragedy. Maybe, Joan thought, but not likely.

Joan had brought a cup of coffee for Susie and a bagel. Joan shook Susie's shoulder and said, "Wake up, sleepyhead, and have your breakfast."

Susie looked up and smiled at her friend, and said, "Thank God it's you. I was worried it was Dr. Harris with bad news." She went on to tell Joan that there was no news but that Greg was staying stable, not talking, and not really aware but alive—thank God."

Joan told her that that was great news; no change was not a bad thing. A heart attack took time; he needed to rest and heal. She also told her friend that she needed to rest before she ended up in a hospital bed. She wanted to know if Susie had slept at all other than in a chair. Susie said no, but she was getting attached to the chair. Susie also told her that Mark was really not talking to her; he had not explained where he was on Friday night, and why he was spending so much time in the city. She told Joan that she thought he had a little somebody on the side, but since she did too, she couldn't call Mark on it. How could she call the kettle black, so to speak?

Joan told her that hopefully things would work out with Mark, and if not then it would be what it would be. But they could talk about Mark and Jay later; right now, all that mattered was Greg getting well. Joan gave Susie a hug and told her that she had to go to work.

Joan caught a glimpse of Frank as he walked into ICU, and he came over to her for a minute and told her to meet him for lunch at noon in the cafeteria. He needed to check on Greg and his other patients, but he looked forward to seeing Joan even for just a short while every day.

CHAPTER 42

Barb

Barb had been devastated to hear about Greg on Saturday. She thought this could have been her family, one of her daughters. Lacey was sixteen, and she was troubled. What if she got into drugs? Maybe she was already involved in drugs. She knew she had to ask Lacey. She had to find out before something awful happened to her daughter.

Barb had planned to spend Saturday with the girls—either the movies, bowling, or shopping. The girls loved to make brownies with her or decorate cookies. She wanted to spend quality time with the girls and let them know that she was always there for them. Jack was gone as usual. He had said he was going fishing with his friends, but most likely he would end up drinking with his cronies.

She called the girls down to the kitchen and said, "Okay, ladies, what it will be today? Movies, bowling, shopping, followed by making homemade pizza and brownies? I'm all yours. Name your game."

Brenda and Rachel both said bowling and yes to brownies. Lacey said, "No thanks, Mom, I have homework. And then I'll do my nails. If you need help with the brownies, I'm glad to help. But I don't feel like going out."

Joan asked Lacey if she had heard about Greg, that he was in the hospital after suffering a heart attack from possibly using drugs. Joan knew the kids shared some of the same friends, and she was curious if Lacey had heard anything or maybe knew something about Greg's friends. Did the kids at school know if Greg was into drugs?

Lacey told her mom that she had heard that Greg was hanging with an older, tougher crowd. But no, she hadn't heard anything about drugs. She and Greg traveled in a totally different crowd. Frankly, lately Lacey wasn't traveling in any crowd, or spending anytime with friends. Lacey had become a loner, but her mother didn't need to know that. She told her mom that she was sorry for Greg and how worried his parents must be.

Barb spent the afternoon with Rachel and Brenda bowling, and then they came home to make the brownies and pizza. The girls loved to roll out the pizza crust, and Rachel liked to make faces on her pizza with olives. Lacey did come down to the kitchen and helped with the brownies. Lacy was trying to reassure her mother; she didn't want her mother to worry about her too. Her mother worked so hard, and she didn't need additional worries.

Jack didn't make it home for dinner, but Barb and the girls had a relaxed meal, and after the dishes were done they sat down for a game of Monopoly. Jack staggered in at nine and wanted to know where his dinner was. Joan offered to heat him up some pizza and add a salad. "What the hell, Barb, don't you have something better for dinner than pizza? What have you been doing all day? I expect a good meal on the table when I get home. I can get pizza anywhere."

Barb tried to tell Jack that it was homemade pizza and brownies that the girls had made, and they were proud of their efforts. Jack just gave Barb a cold look and said, "I don't give a rat's ass who made the pizza. I want a steak or some kind of meat. Now get your ass in the kitchen and make me something edible."

Barb sent the girls upstairs to their room and told Jack that she would try to find something else for him, but if he had wanted a real dinner, then he should have been home at six. She didn't want to start a fight with Jack. It would just upset the girls, and he would get meaner and louder. Better just to find him something to eat and let him sleep it off.

She found some frozen cube steaks in the freezer, thawed two in the microwave, and then fried them up with mushroom and made a red-wine gravy and poured it over mashed potatoes. She called Jack to the table when dinner was ready. While Jack was eating, she told Jack about Greg to change the subject.

Jack told her he didn't give a s—t about Greg and his snotty, uppity parents Susie and Mark. He thought they were both snobs, and maybe if they'd been better parents, their son wouldn't be into drugs. Then he went on to tell her about when he was growing up and how his parents had run a tight ship, always knew what their kids were doing and who they were with. "My parents raised good kids. We all turned out well."

Yeah right, Barb thought, *look at how you turned out.* She just kept her mouth shut and cleaned up the kitchen and headed up to bed. Jack went into the living room and quickly passed out on the couch. *Another exciting Saturday night in my life,* Barb thought to herself.

Sunday passed pretty much the same way as Saturday, but Barb put a roast in the Crock-Pot early. She was not going to be caught without meat again. Jack mowed the lawn and then told Barb that he was going to play pool with some of the guys from work. Barb gave Susie a call at the hospital and then suggested to the girls that after their chores they work on a puzzle.

Lacey did join them for a few hours, and then she quietly returned to her room. At six when dinner was ready Jack still wasn't home, but Barb and the girls ate without him. At least she had roast leftover in the Crock-Pot, so Jack could have a hot meal when he got home if he chose to eat it. When he wasn't home by midnight, Barb went out to turn on the outside lights for Jack and found him lying on the lawn. His car wasn't in the driveway, so he must have walked home. Thank God he hadn't driven, she thought. She decided to leave him on the lawn. It wasn't that cold of a night, and he wouldn't freeze. And if he did, so be it. She really didn't care. She also knew she couldn't take much more. *Why, God? Why me?* she prayed. She always prayed, and so far it hadn't helped. Or maybe God was tired of listening to her. She just went to bed. She was sure that Jack would yell about this tomorrow. What kind of a wife left her husband on the lawn?

Monday morning, Jack had left for work before Barb and the girls got up for breakfast. Jack had made coffee and left a blanket on the couch so at least Barb knew that he had not frozen to death on the lawn. Barb was glad that he had already left because she had nothing to say to him; it had all been said.

Barb dropped Lacey and Brenda off at the high school, and then she and Rachel went on to the elementary school. Barb hoped that being with her students would buoy her spirits. Normally, just being in the classroom made her feel better, and she loved every one of her young students. She intended to have a serious talk with Jack when she got home tonight. Enough was enough. Either he get help or move the hell out of the house. That decided, she was ready to start her day with a lighter heart.

Lacey was dreading her last class of the day, when Mr. Martin stopped her. He told Lacey to wait a minute, that he wanted to go over a test paper with her. Some of the other students looked at Lacey. They were beginning to think that Lacey was either the teacher's pet or always in trouble, but all knew that she stayed late after class at least once a week.

Lacey said, "Please, Mr. Martin, I need to get home. I have to watch my little sisters. Please just let me go."

"Not so fast," Mr. Martin said, as he grabbed Lacey's arm. "You know our agreement. You keep me happy, and your mother keeps her job. Now don't be difficult. You should try to enjoy this more. I certainly do."

He pulled Lacey over, unzipped his pants, and pushed her hand down into his pants. Lacey just turned her head away. She felt sick to her stomach. How much more could she take of this? Maybe she would be better off dead than putting up with this pervert.

Sandy was just walking down the hall of the school. She wanted to catch Lacey before she left the school and hopefully find a place to have a talk to find out the truth. When Sandy peered in the door, she saw the male teacher unzip his pants and grab Lacey's hand and make her touch him. *Oh my god*, she thought, *so this is it, the secret—this disgusting man.* Sandy pulled out her cell phone and took a picture;

she would need proof. Once she had taken the picture, she stormed inside the room and told the man to get his damn hands off Lacey.

She walked up to him and stood with him face-to-face and said, "What the hell do you think you're doing with this young girl, a student? You are a pervert. And how the hell long has this been going on? I am going to your principal and then the police, and you will be arrested for molesting a minor. And I'm pretty sure that Lacey is not your first victim."

Mr. Martin glared back at Sandy and told her that no one would believe her, that she was just a hysterical young woman making accusations, and he was a well-respected teacher. But Sandy told him that if they didn't believe her words, then they would believe her photo and showed him the picture on her phone. She then grabbed Lacey's arm and led her out of the room.

Once outside, Lacey just collapsed on a bench and burst into tears. Sandy put her arms around Lacey and told her that it was all over. That this very sick man could never hurt her again. Sandy then used her cell phone to call the police and asked them to please meet her at the school. She had a case of child abuse to report.

While they waited for the police, Sandy asked Lacey how long this had been going on, and why didn't she say something to her parents or the police? Lacey explained that Mr. Martin had threatened to have her mother fired and ruin her family's reputation. Sandy explained that the teacher really didn't have that kind of power, but she understood why Lacey had been so afraid. Sandy then asked Lacey if this was why she had been cutting herself. Lacey looked startled and then ashamed, but Sandy told her that she had seen her arm one day and suspected the cutting, and she could understand why Lacey had taken up this terrible habit.

Once the police arrived, Sandy explained the situation and told them Mr. Martin's name and room number. One officer stayed with Lacey and Sandy while the other officer went to Mr. Martin's office. The officer with Sandy and Lacey explained that they would prefer to have one of Lacey's parents in attendance, since she was a minor. Sandy placed a call to Barb's cell phone and quickly explained the situation and asked her to come to the high school.

The officer that had checked out Mr. Martin's office came back and told Lacey and Sandy that Mr. Martin was gone, and his desk drawers were open and looked like they had been cleaned out. The officer had stopped by the principal's office and had gotten Mr. Martin's home address and phone number. The principal was shocked at the suggestion that one of his teachers might be a pedophile.

By the time Barb had arrived at the school, the officers and the girls had been joined by the principal. The officers were writing down Lacey's story after Sandy showed them the picture that she had captured with her phone. Lacey told the whole sick story while trying to hold back her sobbing. Her mother just folded Lacey in her arms and said, "Oh baby, I am so sorry. I wish you would have told us. What you have been going through, no wonder you have been so upset. My god, any woman, let alone a child, would be sickened by this bastard's behavior." She turned to the officers. "So now can you arrest him?"

The officers said they would send officers to Mr. Martin's home, and Lacey would need to sign a statement once the full story was down on paper. One of the officers pulled Barb aside and told Barb that Lacey should probably talk to a counselor, a professional; she had been the victim of abuse and would need some help dealing with it. Barb totally agreed, and she said she already had a professional in mind. Barb asked the officer if she could take Lacey home. The officer told her absolutely, but they would like her to come by the station the next day to read and sign a statement, and she should be accompanied by a parent.

Barb put her arm around Lacey and told her that she was taking her home. Barb turned to Sandy and said, "I don't know how to thank you for your bravery and tenacity in finding the truth and exposing this horrible man. I wonder how many young girls have had to suffer under his hands. I hope they find him and put him away for years. Oh, Sandy, I just can't thank you enough." She gave Sandy a big hug as she walked with Lacey to her car. Barb drove Lacey home and told her to lie down if she chose, and Barb went into the other room to call Dr. Andrews and ask if she could bring Lacey in for a joint appointment on Wednesday night. Dr. Andrews absolutely agreed and told Barb to not push Lacey to tell all but tread gently even though she knew that the police had to know the full story. Unfortunately, Dr. Andrews had seen more of these abuse cases than she could stomach.

Brenda and Rachel asked Barb why Lacey was so upset. Had something happened at school? Had a teacher been mean to Lacey? Yes, Barb told them, a very bad teacher had been mean to Lacey. But no more, because the teacher would no longer be teaching at the school.

Barb was waiting to tell Jack when he got home, but when he did come home well after eight, he was in no condition to understand anything she had to tell him. And if he did understand, he might do something crazy and get himself arrested. She knew it was time to tell Jack to get out. She and the girls had suffered enough verbal abuse from Jack, and it was time to move on. She and the girls needed to heal. It was going to take time, but she was determined that she and the girls deserved a better life, with happiness. Enough was enough, time to make a future without Jack in it.

Maggie

Maggie was excited to have her whole family together for break-fast on Sunday morning. Jeff had told his parents that he had asked Michael to drive down for Sunday brunch, using the excuse that he missed his brother, and after hearing the terrible news about Greg being hospitalized, he had suggested that the family needed a bit of together time.

Michael arrived at the house at ten fifteen on Sunday morning and gave everyone a big hug. He said he had stopped at the local bakery to pick up maple bars and an assortment of doughnuts. He told them that no other bakery in the world could make maple bars the way their local bakery did.

Michael gave Jeff a big hug and asked, "Hey, kid, are you ready for this? I've got your back, but don't rush the folks. Let them have time to absorb the news. The folks are pretty cool. They'll come around, but it may take them a little time to adjust. By the way, how is Greg? I was shocked to hear the news that he had a drug-induced heart attack."

Jeff told Michael that it had been touch and go with Greg, but it looked like he was going to make it but would definitely need to go into drug rehabilitation. He told Michael that they hadn't located the other gang members or the guy or pusher providing the drugs, but the police were certainly looking into it.

When the four family members had almost finished breakfast, Jeff told his family that he wanted to talk to them, and to please not ask any questions or interrupt until he was done. Both his parents looked surprised but were not worried. They thought he was going to announce a new girlfriend or a choice of college he wanted to attend. Jeff had always been the easy one, the good one, while Michael had given them a run for their money. Both were great kids, and they were so lucky that their sons were not lying in the hospital from drug addiction.

"Okay, here goes," Jeff said. "I wanted to let you know that I'm pretty sure I'm gay, a homosexual, and I wanted to let you know. I'm not ready to come out yet at school. But I thought you should know, so that you don't push me to date girls, go to proms, or hang out with the neighbor girls. I had talked to Michael about this a few months ago but asked him to keep my secret until I was sure. I am sure now, or mostly sure. I did try to be intimate with a girl, and it just wasn't for me. And then I did try it again with a very nice guy, and it was my wake-up call, and it proved to me what I've been suspecting for the last few years. I was careful and used protection, but I had to know. I couldn't go on like this, thinking I was a freak. Please don't hate me. It would kill me if you can't accept me."

Maggie just gasped and, with tears running down her eyes, turned to Jeff. "If you're sure this is what you want or the life you want to live, then I'm okay with it. It's going to be hard for you, and not everyone is going to understand or be kind, but I will always love and support you. I just want you to be safe. As a pharmacist, I see too many prescriptions for AIDS sufferers, infections, or other sexually transmitted diseases. So please be smart and careful. I will keep your secret until you are ready to truly come out to your friends."

Jeff then looked at his dad. "Well, Dad, what do you think?"

Tom was flabbergasted. In his worse dreams, he had never anticipated having a gay son. Tom had always thought himself a man's man, an athlete and ladies' man in college. How could he have sired a gay son, a fag? What would others think of him? Tom said, "Honestly, Jeff, I'm shocked. And I'm not sure I can accept this. I love you, but I think you must be wrong. Maybe you're just not ready yet, or you're a late bloomer. I can't even imagine or visualize you having sex with another man. Frankly, it makes me sick." Tom then stood up, threw his napkin on the floor, and walked outside.

Jeff was in tears, heartbroken at his Father's cruel words. Now what? Should he move out? Where would he go? he thought. Maggie stood up and came around the table to take Jeff into her arms. She told Jeff that his dad would get over it. "He was just in shock, give him a little time.'

Michael had to agree with his mom and told Jeff, "It's a lot for Dad to accept. He just wants the best for you, we all do. He'll get over it. Just let him think about it for a while. Why don't you come up to Sacramento with me next weekend, and we can hang out? There's a new pizza place I'd like to take you to, and we can go bowling. Just let Dad be for a while, he'll get over it. Ultimately, he'll be proud of you, I certainly am. It takes courage to go in your own direction to follow your own heart, even if it's not the most popular direction. In the meantime, squirt, how about you and I go for a ride and talk a little more. I want to hear more about Greg and his mess."

Jeff agreed, and he and Michael left while Maggie sat down in a chair and sobbed. Never in her wildest dreams could she believe that one of her handsome sons would be gay. Was it something she or Tom had done? Had they not shown a good example of a married couple? Their relationship had been strained lately. What if Tom didn't accept Jeff and drove him out of the house?

Maggie went looking for Tom, but his car was gone. Well, she thought, maybe he just needed to get away and think this through. Hopefully Tom would come to his senses and not drive his son away. She would have a long talk with Tom when he got home; they needed to show a united front to their youngest son.

Tom had headed for one of the bars on Main Street. He normally didn't go to one of these places alone and never in the afternoon, but he had felt suffocated with Jeff's news. He felt like he couldn't breathe; he just had to get away. He kept thinking, *My son is gay. My son is gay, and he'll never have children.* How could Maggie just roll over and accept this? What was wrong with his wife? Didn't she care anymore about his feelings? And why wasn't she supporting him?

Tom spotted Jack and some of his buddies sitting at the end of the bar. *Great*, he thought, *I don't want to get into a conversation with Jack. I certainly don't want him to know about my son.* Tom turned his head away so Jack wouldn't spot him, but unfortunately, too late, Jack was lumbering over to where Tom was sitting.

"So, Tom," Jack said, "this is the last place I thought I would ever see you at. Are you slumming? Trouble in paradise? You, the big fancy dentist in a joint like this. What's going on, Tom? Maggie giving you a bad time? Barb is always on my ass, and the four women are inseparable. Maybe Barb is rubbing off on Maggie. What do you think?" Then Jack gave Tom a wink and a shove on the arm. Jack continued, "Would you like some company? I'd be willing to let you buy me a drink and hear your troubles."

Tom stood up, pulled his arm away, and told Jack, "No, thank you, another time maybe." And Tom walked out of the bar. Jack just watched Tom walk out and thought, *There goes another unhappy SOB. Even a wealthy dentist has problems.*

CHAPTER 44

Susie

By Monday morning, Greg was feeling better but still didn't want to talk about what had happened. He couldn't admit to himself or his parents that he had a drug problem. The doctors had told him that he had been lucky, but he would need to stay in the hospital another week or so, and then they suggested a rehab program.

Susie had stayed with Greg throughout the weekend, and Mark had left that morning to go back to San Francisco. He told Susie that he had a responsibility to his clients, but he would return to the hospital that night. Susie tried to get Greg to tell her where he had been getting the drugs and the names of his new friends, but Greg had been adamant that he was not going to squeal on his friends. Greg was also disappointed that none of his new friends had come to visit him in the hospital. Maybe, he thought, they just hadn't heard yet. He couldn't believe that these guys would just ignore him, and he wanted to let them know that he wasn't going to rat them out or give out names. It wasn't their fault that he had mixed too many drugs or maybe took too many. He really couldn't remember much about Friday night.

Jay had continued to call Susie to check on Greg, and he had taken the day off work on Monday to follow up on his hunt for the drug pusher. He had heard some names on Sunday and wanted to check out a guy by the name of Shane, whose name kept coming up in association with gang activity. He had heard that Shane, being a high school dropout, hung out at the local pool hall.

Jay walked into the pool hall around one. He ordered a beer and then walked over to a pool table and asked the guys at the table if they'd like to play a game for a little cash. A couple of the guys said they were in, and the balls were racked and the game started. After a brief time, Jay brought up the question of where he might find a buy of street drugs. Jay told them that he was new to town, and he just needed a new contact. He was willing to pay well and would compensate anyone that would help set him up.

The other two guys were leery at first, but after Jay bought them a couple of beers and after three more games of pool, the guys were feeling more comfortable with Jay, and they thought that Jay seemed like a regular guy. He also seemed to be flush with cash as he continued to buy them beers.

One of the guys told him that a guy named Shane seemed to be in the know and had a source. Jay said great and asked where he might find Shane. The guy told him that Shane was a regular, and he usually came into the pool hall every afternoon around four or so. Jay thanked the guys and gave them twenty dollars each for their kindness. "Hey, anytime, dude." They laughed.

Jay called Susie after he left the pool hall. He said he had kept hearing the name Shane associated with drug sales. He suggested that Susie casually mention the name Shane to Greg to see how he reacts. Jay thought he was on the right track, and he wasn't going to quit until he found the dealer. He told Susie that he loved her, and if he couldn't be with her, he would want to help bring down the bastards that had almost killed her son. He said he would keep her informed.

When Susie casually asked Greg if he had a friend named Shane, her son's face turned white, and he turned his head away. Finally, Greg said, "I don't think so. Why? Have you heard something?"

Susie told him no, but she thought Sandy or Lacey had mentioned his name as somebody that dealt in drug deals. She told him that she was just curious if he knew him, no problem. She didn't want to push Greg in his weakened condition.

That afternoon, at four, Jay was back at the pool hall and asked around for a guy named Shane. A tall and skinny guy with black stringy hair approached Jay and said, "That might be me, depending on what you want and who wants to know."

Jay told the same story that he was new to town and needed a little help obtaining a small supply of street drugs. He said he was willing to pay handsomely and laid a one-hundred-dollar bill on the bar in front of Shane. Jay told Shane that he was a truck driver, and every once in a while, he needed a little "pick me up" when he had a cross-country haul. Would Shane maybe know of someone he could hook Jay up with?

Shane told him that he wasn't sure, but maybe he could find a source. He asked Jay to wait a few minutes while he made a call, and just maybe he could help him out. When Shane came back into the room after five minutes, he picked up the one hundred dollars off the table and told him to meet him at Joe's garage on Brown Street at six.

"I think my friend can help you out."

"Great," Jay said, "I'll see you then. Thanks for helping me out, Shane."

When Jay left the pool hall, he went directly to the police department on Main Street. He asked to speak to someone on the force who was dealing with local illegal drug sales. Jay was introduced to Officer Laird, who told Jay that he knew there was someone locally pushing street drugs to teenage kids, but so far he hadn't been able to get any names or nail anyone down. Jay told the officer about Greg being in the hospital and that he had started snooping around and had found a name and had then made an appointment to buy some drugs at six that night at Joe's garage.

Jay said, "I think it would be a very good idea if you could have an officer hidden close by in case the deal goes down. I would be glad to wear a wire if it would help nail the bastard."

Officer Laird said he would be there himself with backup and would wire Jay up. He also told Jay that what he was doing was dangerous and was he sure that he wanted to get involved? Jay told Officer Laird that someone he cared a great deal about had almost lost her son, and he wanted to help in the only way he could, and that was to put the dealers out of business.

While Jay was in St. Helena trying to find Greg's friends and pushers, Mark was back in San Francisco telling Kim his story of woes. Kim put her arms around Mark and said, "You poor baby. What a terrible weekend you must have had. Where was your wife in all this, when your son was becoming a drug addict? Doesn't she watch her son at all? You can't be expected to do it all, work in the city and then run home to check on your son. What kind of a mother is she anyway? I don't know how you have put up with this for so long."

Mark felt that Kim knew exactly what he was going through. She was empathetic and understanding and assured Mark that a man can't do it all, and his wife should have been watching for signs that something was off with Greg.

But no, Mark thought, *Susie was too busy playing bocce and making wine.* Mark felt totally unappreciated and very righteous in his indignation. He was going to have a heart-to-heart talk with Susie, and she had better shape up, or he was shipping out. Kim was waiting in the wings, and she was much more understanding than Susie. He wasn't sure that he wanted to do the long haul with Greg and rehabilitation; Susie could just deal with it. After all, he had done the best he could. What more did they expect of him?

Jay walked into the garage promptly at six. Shane was inside and introduced Jay to Frankie. Frankie, Jay noted, was probably in his midthirties with long blondish hair, and he was maybe twenty pounds overweight. Obviously, he didn't indulge in what he sold. Shane seemed nervous, but Frankie just appeared arrogant and self-confident. Frankie said, "So, Jay, what's your pleasure? Uppers, downers, pot, or cocaine?"

Jay told him that he needed some amphetamines to keep awake on long hauls. He was a trucker and needed something to perk him up through the nights. Jay pulled out five hundred dollars and held it out to Frankie and told him to give him whatever that would buy.

Once the envelope containing the pills and the money exchanged hands, Officer Laird and another officer walked into the garage and told Frankie and Shane they were under arrest for possession and selling of illegal drugs. Frankie turned to Shane, "What the hell! You set me up? I thought I could trust you. But no, you little punk, you brought the cops right to my door. I will take you down, no matter how long it takes. I will find you and take you down."

Jay looked at Shane and Frankie and said, "This is for my friend Greg who almost died from a drug-induced heart attack, thanks to you guys. So now you both will pay for all the damage you have done to the young people in this town."

The officer told Jay that Shane also looked like the description of the teenagers that had robbed the liquor store the other night. But they would question Shane about that later.

As soon as Jay was free, he called Susie at the hospital to tell her that Greg's friend Shane and the pusher Frankie had been arrested, and it was just a matter of time before the other gang members were rounded up. He asked if he could meet with her in the next few days, even if only for a few minutes. He wanted her to know that he would always be there for her.

Susie waited until the next morning and then told Greg that his friends Shane and Frankie had been arrested for possession and selling of illegal drugs. Greg looked in his mom's eyes and broke down. He told her that he had wanted to quit but didn't know how. He told her that he had been a fool and had stolen liquor and some of her jewelry to support his habit. He told her where the pawnshop was, so she could buy back her ring and broach. He said, "I'm so sorry, Mom. I was a fool. I thought they were fun, cool guys. I was an idiot. I will go to rehab. it that's what you want. I am so sorry, please forgive me."

Susie gave Greg a hug and told him that yes, he did need to go into rehab, and he was lucky to be alive. She told him that everyone made stupid mistakes, that it was part of growing up. "I love you, Greg, and I will always love you. I forgive you. And I will buy back my jewelry, even though it was kind of ugly. But it was my Mother's, so I know she would roll over in her grave if I didn't. You have learned a hard lesson, but so have I. And it's time our family got their s—t together. I also have a friend that I would like you to meet one of these days. I think you'll like him."

CHAPTER 45

Joan

Joan got home from the hospital on Monday at four and checked on the roast that she had put in the Crock-Pot. All she had to do was add the carrots and potatoes, toss a salad and frost the cake, and she was ready for a family dinner. They hadn't seen Brad for a few weeks, and Sandy was anxious to tell her brother about her bust of Mr. Martin Lacey's teacher. She had told the story over and over again to her parents. She had said, "You should have seen the look on Mr. Martin's face when I confronted him with the picture of him assaulting Lacey." Sandy was now considering a job as a detective or police officer instead of nursing.

"And tomorrow," her mother told her, "you'll want to be a pilot. One day at a time, kiddo."

Sandy and Bob both walked in the door at five thirty, and Brad was due by six. When six thirty came and went, Joan was getting worried. Bob tried to convince her that Brad was fine and just running late, but after trying his cell phone and getting no response, Bob was starting to worry too.

At seven fifteen, a local sheriff knocked on their door and told Joan and Bob that he was so sorry, but Brad had been in a motorcycle accident. He was alive but barely. He had been riding his motorcycle when he had been forced off the road by a tourist driving too fast. Brad's bike had gone into the vineyards where he had hit his head on a grape stake. Apparently, he had been wearing a helmet, but it was not hooked and it had come off at impact. Brad was at the St. Helena

Hospital, and the officer would be glad to drive them if they were too upset to drive.

"Oh my god," Joan said. "Brad. How could this happen? I told you I hate motorcycles, and now this one may kill my son."

Bob just grabbed Joan's arm and told her that they needed to go to the hospital, and she should ride with the sheriff, and he and Sandy would follow in his car. Bob felt an overwhelming sense of guilt. *Joan is right*, he thought, *I should have told him to get rid of the bike too. But no, I had told him to go ahead. That Joan was just overreacting. What a fool I've been, what a damn fool.*

He and Sandy followed the sheriff's car to the hospital. When Joan arrived at the hospital, she was told that Brad was alive but had suffered a head trauma, and the emergency room doctor told her that a neurologist had been called it. Brain scans were being done, and they were waiting for the specialists. She was told that Brad had a fractured arm and lacerations, but their biggest worry was the brain trauma.

Sandy and Bob arrived a few minutes later to find Joan sobbing. She told both of them what she had been told—that Brad had a brain trauma, and they were waiting for a neurologist, but the outcome didn't look good. Brad's vitals were weak, and he was barely hanging on. Sandy suggested to her mom that she call Dr. Harris. Even though he was a cardiologist, he could help with the doctor's translations and be there if anything else came up with Brad. "Mom, you trust Dr. Harris. I think we need him here now."

Joan tearfully agreed and asked the nurse to call Dr. Harris at home and explain the situation and ask him to come in. All they could do now was wait. Joan had seen these terrible accidents before, and she knew the odds of Brad's survival.

Frank arrived at the hospital in ten minutes and went right into the emergency room to find out what he could before he would face Joan and her family. The emergency room doctor didn't have good news for Frank and told him that he was worried about swelling in the brain. The neurologist had just arrived and was examining Brad.

Frank went out to the waiting room and gave Joan a hug and introduced himself to Bob and Sandy. He told them that the neurologist was on-site and was with Brad, and hopefully they would know more soon. He said the other injuries were not that severe, but it was the head trauma that they were concerned with. Frank tried to assure them that Brad was young and strong and, God willing, would survive this. He was glad to stay and pitch in if needed.

After almost two hours, the neurologist came out to talk to the family. Dr. Wilson told them that the good news was that Brad was still alive, although from the brain scans it looked like Brad had a subdural hematoma, and there was brain swelling. If the swelling didn't start to go down in the next few hours, they would perform a burr hole and drain the fluid or blood that was pressing against the brain. They were keeping Brad in a drug-induced coma.

Joan asked if Brad still had signs of brain activity or could he be brain dead? She could barely get the words out between sobs. Dr. Wilson said from what he could determine there definitely was brain activity, but only time would tell if Brad survived and if he would have any permanent or lingering damage. The doctor then told them how much he hated motorcycles and the terrible waste and damaged souls he had seen from these stupid machines.

Bob just collapsed into a chair, saying, "It's my fault. You warned me, Joan, and I didn't listen. If that boy dies or is permanently damaged, it's my fault. I could have stopped him, but I didn't. My macho male self was actually jealous that my son would have all the fun with his new bike. I had always wanted one when I was young, and my mother and dad wouldn't let me have one. What an idiot I am. I'm so sorry, Joan, so sorry."

Sandy just sat down and held her dad's hand. She said, "Not now, Dad. There will be plenty of time for recriminations, but now we just have to pray and be strong for Brad."

Joan just looked at Bob. She wasn't sure if she was angrier with Bob or Brad, but she just couldn't deal with it now. She couldn't even look at Bob; the pain in her heart was too great. Did she blame Bob? Maybe she didn't know. Bob had always been too busy lately to even deal with his family. She was sure he was hurting, but where had he been when his family needed him? At the store, always the damn store.

The wait seemed endless, until Dr. Wilson came back in to see them and tell them the swelling wasn't going down and that they needed to drill a burr hole right away. They were prepping Brad for the procedure right now. Joan asked if they could see Brad just for a minute. Dr. Wilson told them they could peek in for two minutes. "And I do mean two minutes."

Joan and Bob went into the room and were shocked with what they saw. Brad's head was bandaged, and tubes were running into his arm; his color was gray. Joan, who was used to seeing patients looking like this, was horrified when she saw her son lying there so still. She just touched Brad's hand, said a quiet prayer, and then left the room. Bob gave Brad a kiss on the cheek and then followed Joan out.

Joan then went up to the chapel to pray. Bob just sat in a chair with his head buried in his hands. He didn't feel like he had the right to talk to God; he had failed his son and his wife.

Sandy had called Barb to check on Lacey and told Barb about Brad's accident. Barb was floored. So much had happened in just the last few days: first Greg, then Lacey, and now Brad. Barb wasn't aware of Jeff, since Maggie and Tom were keeping Jeff's secret.

Barb called Susie on her cell phone at the hospital and then Maggie at home. She wanted everyone to pray for Brad. Susie said she would go downstairs to the emergency room. Greg was asleep. The other two friends said they would come to the hospital to hold the vigil with Joan and her family. Barb told them, "We won't bother them but just be there to pray. The more prayers shared, the more likely they'll be heard."

The three friends gathered in the waiting room; gave Joan, Sandy, and Bob a hug; and then quietly settled down on a couch on the other side of the room. Frank came back to check on Joan. He had been in and out of the room with Brad, watching the procedure. He told Joan and Bob that everything was going fine. So far Brad was holding his own. Joan then quickly introduced her friends to Frank.

Jay called in to check on Susie again, and when she hung up, she explained that Jay had helped the police catch the drug pushers that had been supplying the drugs to the kids. The ladies were amazed, and Barb said, "Wow, Jay, what a stud. Not only is he young and handsome, but he's also a detective on the side. Wonder where he keeps his badge?"

The others laughed and Frank said, "Wait, fill me in. Who's dealing drugs? Who's Jay? What, drugs in this sleepy little town?"

Susie proceeded to tell Frank about Jay's determination to find the guys selling the drugs that had caused Greg's heart attack, and that he had succeeded, and they had been arrested. Barb interrupted and said, "Yes, and Jay—Susie's friend—rode in to the rescue to avenge her son and his pushers. What a guy."

Frank told the ladies that he was duly impressed with Jay's sleuthing and then said he was going to the cafeteria for a coffee. He asked if anyone else wanted to go. Barb agreed to go; she was ready for a break.

Once Frank and Barb settled down over a cup of coffee, Barb shared her story of Lacey and the horrendous weekend the three women had shared. "Who could believe it?" she said, "three of us with all this drama in one weekend."

Frank told her that sometimes that was just the way it happened. "You go along fine and then boom, the s—t hits the fan all at one time."

Over the next hour, Frank told Barb about his deceased wife and what a lifeline Joan had thrown him and what a friend she had turned out to be. Frank asked Barb if she was married, and she told him for now, but that was soon to change. She then explained about her husband's alcoholism and his refusal to deal with it. She told Frank she was done; she just had to tell Jack when he was sober enough to listen. When they went back to the waiting room, they both felt like old friends.

Dr. Wilson finally came out after another hour and told them that Brad had come through the procedure well, and now time would tell. The next few days would be critical. He told the family that they could go home if they chose, but Joan and Bob insisted on staying. Sandy said she would go home and feed the cat and told her parents to call if there was any change.

Susie went back upstairs to stay with Greg, and Maggie and Barb went home. Maggie needed to talk to Tom about his response to Jeff, and Barb wanted to talk to Jack and tell him to start packing. A lot had happened to them over the weekend that would cause permanent changes in their lives.

Bob and Joan just sat in silence for most of the night. When Bob reached for Joan's hand, she just pulled it away. She just couldn't deal with his sorrow and hers at the same time. The pain was just too great.

CHAPTER 46

Barb

Jack was watching a fight on TV when Barb got home from the hospital. The girls were upstairs in Lacey's room. Brenda and Rachel had talked Lacey into playing a game of Monopoly. Lacey and Brenda had made boxed macaroni and cheese for their dinner. Lacey told her sisters that she had an issue with a male teacher at her school and that he had been fired for his rude behavior. She didn't want to go into the fact that he was a sexual predator, or that the police were still looking for him. Lacey was feeling better just knowing that she would never suffer from Mr. Martin and his disgusting demands ever again.

Barb joined Jack on the couch in the living room and told him that she would like to talk to him for a few minutes. He turned off the TV and told her that she had five minutes; he didn't want to miss the end of the fight. Barb explained what had happened at the school with Lacey and her teacher, Mr. Martin, and that he had been abusing Lacey and exposing himself to her for the last few months. She told Jack that it had actually been Sandy, Joan's daughter, that had discovered it and called the police. The police were looking for Mr. Martin but had not yet located him. The police were also doing background checks on him to see if other complaints had ever been filed against him.

Jack was shocked and upset that someone had tried to hurt his daughter. Jack said, "If I ever get my hands on the SOB, I will kill him. Nobody touches my girls, nobody. Is Lacey okay? Do we need to take her to a doctor?"

Barb told him that she was going to take Lacey to a therapist on Wednesday night. Dr. Andrews was a family counselor and would work with the whole family to deal with the healing process. She also told Jack that it was not just Lacey that needed help, but all of them would benefit from the counseling.

Jack replied that he didn't see the need for him to go; he didn't have any problems. It was fine for Barb and Lacey, but personally he didn't believe in the hocus pocus of therapy for adults. Barb explained to Jack that he needed help with his drinking, and how his drinking was destroying their family.

Jack became irate and started shouting at Barb that he didn't have a problem, she did. He got right in Barb's face, grabbed her arm, and said, "I have a few drinks now and then like all the guys, and you make a huge issue out of it. I'm tired of you being in my face all the time about it. I will drink as much as I want, when I want, and with whom I want. And if you don't like it, tough s—t." He then picked up the bottle of beer that had been lying by the chair and threw it against the wall, spattering broken glass everywhere.

Barb was startled and surprised; Jack had never been physical in his anger before. Verbally abusive, yes, but physically no. Barb stood her ground and told Jack, "I want you out of this house now. I will give you fifteen minutes to pack a bag of clothes and get the hell out of this house, or I will call the sheriff, and you know I will. I have friends in the sheriff's office, and I teach the Sheriff's son, so I know he will get over here in minutes. I am afraid for my life and the girls' lives. And after what Lacey has been through, I'm sure they will be very understanding. So get your ass upstairs, pack, and get the hell out. You can pick up the rest of your stuff on the weekend when the girls and I are out of the house."

Jack could see that Barb was serious and would absolutely carry through on her threat. Jack said, "Fine, I'll go for now, but this isn't over. You'll miss me, and you can't afford to support this house and the girls on your own. You'll come crawling, asking me to come back. And then you'll be sorry when I won't."

Barb stood firm and replied, "Actually, Jack, we'll be fine. I've already talked to our principal about my taking on some private tutoring. So financially, we'll be fine. Things may be tighter, but we'll manage. You will also be obligated to pay child support. I have asked you repeatedly to get help with your drinking, but you won't, so now I'm telling you we're done. I have to put the girls' interests first. So you'd better hurry, Jack, your fifteen minutes is running out."

Jack started up the stairs but told Barb that no one was going to tell him to quit drinking or how to run his life. He would leave for now, but Barb would hear from his lawyer.

Fifteen minutes later, Jack walked out the door with his suitcase, computer, and a bag of beer and whiskey. He left without another word to Barb or the girls.

After Jack left, the girls came down into the living room and put their arms around their mom. Lacey told her mom that she was so sorry if she had caused this rift between her parents. Barb said, "No, Lacey, neither you nor your sisters had anything to do with this. It was all on Dad and his drinking. This has been going on for years, and I should have stood up to him years ago. If I had, maybe things would have been different. Lacey, I think you and I have both learned something. We need to stand up for ourselves. Don't remain silent. Don't put up with predators, whether they're family, friends, or teachers. If we keep quiet, they win. We need to speak up and fight back. Our family is going to be fine, I promise you. Just fine."

CHAPTER 47

Friends

Thursday night six months later, the four friends had just arrived at their favorite after-bocce pub for their usual wine and chat. They were buzzing with excitement; they had just won all three bocce games and were now firmly in second place. Barb said, "We did it, we kicked their ass. Did you see the looks on those guys' faces? They couldn't believe that eight women could outplay them. They didn't have a chance. We were awesome!"

The other three women just laughed at Barb, but were absolutely agreeing with her. Maggie told them how proud she was of the team, and she suggested that they get together and pick a date for a weekend barbecue to celebrate their win and awesome season. Maggie offered to host it at her house; she'd supply the meat, Susie could bring the wine, Joan the salads, and Barb could bring desserts. The ladies agreed that that sounded great, and they deserved a celebration.

Maggie asked if Barb would be bringing a date. She had heard that Barb had been seeing a lot of a certain Dr. Frank Harris. Barb smiled and agreed that she would like to bring Frank. He had become a good friend, and they were seeing each other at least once a week for dinner or a movie. They had discovered interests in common and were enjoying each other's company. Recently their evenings had turned romantic, with more kissing than talking. Barb's divorce would be final in six months, and she was looking forward to being free. Barb's girls really liked Frank, and he would often include them in their evenings, with dinner out, or bowling outings, and trips to the coast. He and the girls had discovered their love of kite flying on the beach. Frank was teaching the girls how to make their own kites. He had unlimited patience when it came to children.

Barb said, "What about you, Susie, will you bring Jay? How are things going between you two? Have you and Mark finally worked out your divorce settlement"?

Susie said yes, that she was still seeing Jay, and he had been wonderful with Greg. Once Greg had gotten out of the six-week rehab program, Jay and Greg had started hanging out together. The guys would go fishing together, and both loved backpacking and camping. Susie had gone camping with them a few times, but her back didn't love sleeping on the ground in sleeping bags. She said, "I guess this is what happens when your boyfriend is sixteen years younger than you. I feel like I'm raising two boys." But she had to admit that Jay was a better dad than Mark was. He was gentle and patient with Greg, and he treated Susie like a queen. The age difference didn't seem to bother Jay, so maybe Susie shouldn't worry about it either.

Susie told the others that she felt bad that Mark still spent very little time with Greg. He'd call once a week and would take him to lunch every two weeks, but other than that the relationship between them was strained. Mark and Kim had broken up, but Mark was still pursuing younger women in the city.

Mark had found a small apartment in San Francisco and was living there full-time. Their attorneys had finally worked out an equitable settlement, and Susie would maintain the house. And with her job, she and Greg would be fine. Greg was doing better too, still seeing a therapist in Calistoga, and was staying clean. His grades were up, and he had found some new friends and had reestablished a relationship with some of his old friends. Shane and his buddies were history and had faced some legal consequences for their drug pushing and petty thefts. Greg had gone to the owner of the liquor store personally apologized and paid for the stolen liquor. Frankie the drug dealer had faced jail time. Susie had been able to purchase her jewelry back from the pawnshop, although it hadn't been inexpensive.

Susie said, "What about you, Maggie? How are things with you and Tom? I know things were touch and go with you two. He was not being warm and cuddly. Are things any better? Will you bring him to the barbecue?"

Maggie said things had gotten better once Tom had calmed down about Jeff. Maggie had told her friends about Jeff once he had given her permission. She said, "I think Tom was feeling old and forgotten, you know midlife crisis. He had just turned fifty-two, and I think he was feeling like life was passing him by. And then he took in Dr. Sharon, the dentist, and I think she was attractive to him at first, flirty and fun. But when she truly started to put the make on him, he ran with his tail between his legs. He finally realized she was trying to become a partner in the practice, and her way up was literally to sleep her way to the top. Once she showed her hand, Tom told her that it wasn't working out and for her to find another practice to go into. Tom is waiting for Michael to come into the practice someday. As for Jeff, he and Tom are working things out slowly. Tom is finding out that gayness is not contagious or an affront to Tom's manhood. Tom had to realize that a person is not judged on their sexuality or if they're attracted to a female or male, but about their self-worth, their kindness, their dignity. Tom knows that Jeff is a good kid. Whether he likes girls or boys, he's still the same sweet guy inside with the same compassion and kindness. Tom just had to remember that, and now the two of them are spending more time together. Michael is coming home more on the weekends to spend time with Jeff. Jeff has not told his friends about being gay yet, but he will when the time is right. He may wait until he goes off to college. It might be easier in a new environment with new friends. But it's his choice, and we will respect his choice. And thank you, ladies, for respecting Jeff's secret. Oh, and Tom has become much more cuddly with me too. I guess I must be looking better to him, after Sharon scared the hell out of him."

Maggie looked at Joan and said, "Okay, kid, tell all."

Joan just smiled. "Okay," she said, "I will tell all. Bob and I finally forgave each other for Brad's accident. I blamed Bob at first for not stopping Brad from buying the damn bike. And I blamed myself for not pushing harder to stop him. Bob and I had grown apart with his shutting me out, him spending more and more time at the store, and I began to respect him less. I let my friendship with Frank—sorry, Barb—take precedence over my marriage. I don't think anything would have ever happened with Frank other than friendship, but still I should have worked harder on my marriage than I did. Brad's accident was a wakeup call for both Bob and I. Bob realized that he had almost lost his family, and now he is working eight-hour days and taking time off during the weekend. We have actually gotten away a few weekends, and it was wonderful. I think we're finding each other again. Brad is doing great, thank God. Those three weeks in the hospital were the toughest of our lives. But Brad is doing fine, with no lingering effects, other than a new shaved head. He actually bought an SUV last weekend. No more bikes or even small cars for Brad. He's also dating a new young woman, Carrie, and she's wonderful. She adores Brad, and we adore her. She's a paralegal in Napa and is very mature and good for Brad, and she loves to cook. A girl after my own heart. Sandy is Sandy, doing her own thing, mothering everyone, being a Nancy Drew, getting good grades, and just enjoying dating a multitude of guys. She's going to make a great nurse. Nothing scares that girl, absolutely nothing. Her dad calls her Salty Sandy, and she is. She will mow you down if you get in her way of saving lost souls or lost causes. I truly love that girl. She's my wild crusading child."

Barb said, "God bless your crusading daughter. She saved my Lacey's life. Lacey finally told me and the therapist about the cutting and her depression. Lacey is doing so much better. She's still seeing Dr. Andrews, but the cutting has stopped. She's gained weight, and she's smiling again. She is also seeing her old friends. What a difference. That terrible man almost destroyed her life and would have if Sandy hadn't intervened. Sandy and Lacey still get together every few weeks for lunch. The girls aren't excited to see their dad, but Jack does call every week or so. He hasn't asked to take them anywhere, and if he sees them, he comes by for a few minutes after work. He did agree to pay child support. And with my teaching and part-time tutoring, we're getting by. I don't know if Jack will ever quit drinking, but that's his problem now, not mine. We are trying to all move on. I know Lacey will have to testify against Mr. Martin one of these days when his case goes to court, and I assume Sandy will also testify. I was so relieved when we heard that the police had caught him trying to cross the Mexican border. Mr. Martin apparently pulled this in other schools, but he had been fired, and the girls had been too frightened to tell their story. I don't think Lacey would have ever stood up and told her story if Sandy hadn't intervened. We'll deal with the court business when it happens, but for now we're doing fine."

Maggie suggested that they invite the other four women of their team and their spouses. She thought it might be nice to get to know the other women better and their families. Friendships should be like grapes—the more grapes on the vine, the better the wine.

Susie said, "Hey, wait, that should have been my line. Remember, I'm the little old winemaker." Susie held up her glass for a toast as the others joined in. "To friendship. May it always have your back, hold you in its arms, and be like a summer breeze, soft and gentle."

CPSIA information can be obtained
at www.ICGtesting.com
Printed in the USA
FSHW011526160621
82415FS